XOXO Allison

R80

STONE

Cover Model: Burton Hughes
Cover Photography: Eric David Battershell
Paperback Cover: Designs by Dana
Editing: Julia Goda
Printed in the United States of America

STONE

By Hilary Storm & Kathy Coopmans

PROLOGUE
HARRIS

She's perfect, and I haven't been able to keep my hands off her since the day I first heard her sassy mouth. Hell, I never knew I needed her until I was blacked out from being shot. Waking up and dreaming of her only solidified that I needed her in my life.

"Come here, baby. Why are you hiding that sexy body?" I call her over to the bed where I've been watching her since our shower together. She's been drying her hair and teasing me all over again while she walks around with a towel tucked around her tits. Not sure why she thinks she has to hide anything from me. I have every inch of her body memorized. The only struggle here should be which part of that full of sin, sweet flesh she wants to let me nibble on first.

Her smile turns seductive just as she drops the towel, only lighting another fire inside me. Her sexy walk toward me gives me the urge to go to her, but I stop myself and just count my blessings and take it all in. This is a life I can get used to. Mallory completes me, and right now in this moment, I can't imagine being any happier or anywhere else.

"You're so damn sexy." I reach for her hand, only to have her beat me to it. She takes control, her tits teasing me as she climbs to position herself and straddles my already hard cock. Her pussy is slick and tight, and I can feel her heat as she glides herself down my shaft.

"I just want to be inside you every..." I thrust upward, going deeper inside her with every word. "Single...Second."

"Oh God, Beau. You make me crazy." Her lip quivers. I love how her body always reacts so passionately to my every move. She's a livewire when I'm with her; it's as if a bright spark goes off from a simple touch when we're together. I've been with her many times and made it my goal to know exactly what she likes. We've definitely found some things she didn't even know she liked, during our journey of familiarizing ourselves with each other.

Mallory likes me deep and she likes it when I take control even though she tried to start in control today. I let her play a little longer before I flip her onto her back and put her legs over my shoulders. I close my eyes and exhale as I roll my hips even deeper.

"Yesss. Just like that." She leans her head back, and I watch her face while she takes my thrusts. I never take it easy on her. She has never let me. Her moans and begging always brings out the hunger in me, until I end up pounding her like I'm fucking for the very last time. Every time I thrust, we move closer to the headboard, sliding up the sheets and getting louder all the way.

If we hadn't already had sex four times today, I'd take my time with her. I do love to savor her even though I like to fuck her hard, but I know we're both dragging-ass tired and need to get our rest before our trip tomorrow. I begin to move faster, taking her legs and spreading them even wider. I listen to her moans rise and increase before she goes silent, bows her back, and comes all over my dick. Her warmth, her love for me is sending me straight into a stupor when I feel her clench tight around me, only making me send my cum straight into her.

I collapse next to her in the bed, pull her against my body, and take our usual position. She always lays her head on my chest, and I always hold her with my arm. It's become the norm. I'm relaxed when her words force me to open my eyes once again.

"I need to talk to you." She grabs my free arm, drags it across my body, and places it against her stomach.

"Okay," I say with hesitation, hoping she isn't going to tell me she needs a break from all of this, because that isn't an option for me.

"How do you feel about moving in together?" I lift my head and think about what she's asking. I've practically stayed at her house since the day I met her, so to me it's as if we live together anyway.

"Sounds good. Your place or mine?" I smirk even though she can't see me. I know exactly where she's going to want to live. I sink my head back into my pillow as I wait for her response.

"Mine. It's bigger. We'll need an extra room for the nursery." My head jerks, my ears echoing her words as I try to comprehend what she just said. I sit up with shock running through my veins, hitting me like a loud whirl of thunder. I roll her onto her back to see if she's joking and try to compose my emotional energy that honestly, I can't even explain. When I notice the tears running down her face in the moonlight, I know she's serious. I shove back the shock and fear and give her the reaction she deserves from me. *Holy fuck!*

"Are you serious?" A smile spreads across my face the second hers lights up and she begins to nod yes while she releases a few sobs. "I can't believe this. We made a tiny human!" She begins to laugh, and I can hear relief in her voice as she slows her movements. I lower myself until my face is over her stomach. Even though in the back of my mind I'm terrified, I'm excited beyond belief that this means I'll forever be tied to this woman.

I place a kiss right above her belly button. "Hello there, little guy." She starts laughing before I finish. "Don't interrupt my one-on-one time with my kid," I say seriously.

"You know it's going to be a girl, so don't even try." She laughs as she tries to pull me up her body. I go willingly, kissing every inch until I come in contact with her lips.

"It doesn't matter, as long as it's healthy…and has a big dick between its legs," I tell her between kisses. She stops and smacks my arm before she attempts to tickle me for the tenth time today. She's determined to prove I'm ticklish when we both know I'm not.

"You'd better stop before you get the dick again. You know what this shit does to me." I laugh at her antics. Call it crazy, but when she gets this way with her hands all over me, it turns me the hell on. She sits over me with a huge smile on her face and her hair hanging over her left shoulder.

"You know that's why I do it, don't you?" Her hands run over my stomach and up my chest before she lies down beside me. I pull her against my body and start thinking about just how different my life will be from this point on.

The crazy thing is, I'm excited as hell about it. This woman is having my baby, and I can't fucking wait to meet this tiny human I created with the woman I love.

CHAPTER ONE

HARRIS

Nine Months Later

"Get up, damn it, Harris. I need your ass moving today." The sound of Kaleb ripping my curtains open pisses me off even more than the sound of his voice does.

"Not in the mood for your bossy ass today, Maverick. Get the fuck out." I've avoided him and the other guys for days, but apparently, he's determined to get up in my face today. I'm not dealing with him and his shit, just like I haven't for days. He can leave me the hell alone.

"I told the Army I'd take care of you, so that's what the fuck I'm going to do. Get up. I want you around the table today. You know we have to put our heads together for this kind of shit. I need all hands on deck, so I'm going to need you to pull your shit together just long enough for us to get a plan." I listen to his loud fucking voice barrel through the room just like it did back in Afghanistan. He needs to remember this is not the fucking desert and I'm not going to do every damn thing he wants me to just because he demands it. Those days are over.

I scoot against the headboard and run my fingers through my hair while I bite my tongue. I have to. What I really want to say to him, I know he doesn't deserve. That's the problem, there's no one to blame.

"How many times do I have to tell you I don't know anything? This shit is not my expertise. I don't analyze shit. I fucking attack. You get me the damn information and then leave me the fuck alone to handle business once you know something." I feel my heart contract with my words and can't seem to shake the overwhelming desire to want to kill someone more each day. Hell, I need to do something very soon or the tiny fragment of my mind that's still functioning is going to erupt, leaving me without a care in the fucking world. Not that I give a shit about a damn thing as it is.

"Right. You've said that. And you also told me you needed a few days before you'd get your ass out there. Well, it's been a few fucking weeks."

"You're right. Excuse me for taking a few extra days to deal with shit that I need to deal with." I yell, then throw the covers off of me and storm into the bathroom, slamming the door behind me. *Fuck him.*

"Shit," I mumble as I lose my footing on the rug. I feel dizzy as fuck, and the pressure in my chest starts building again from the thought of helping them. If I hadn't already dealt with this time and time again, I'd swear I was having a heart attack. Pain shoots across my back and down my arm before I can get another breath out. The thought of trying to be normal again is making me crazy. I feel like I'm about to explode. I want out of here.

I hurry to take a piss, then grab my shorts from the floor and slide them on over my boxers. I need to fucking run. I need to feel the air in my chest before I fucking blow up from this stress and anxiety of the damn panic attack that is heavily circling me.

When I open the door to find Maverick still sitting on the edge of the bed, it doesn't make me feel any better. "Look," he says. "I know this shit is hard, but you have to take the first step. Getting out of bed today can be your first step." I can't look at him. The last thing I want to do is show any more emotion about anything. I've already lost my shit a few times as I've been trying to figure out how to keep from drowning in the depths of blackness.

"Alright, I'm up. So mission fucking accomplished today. Will you leave me the fuck alone now?"

"Harris." His voice is laced with sympathy, and his eyes mirror the same haunting expression I see when I look at my own on the days I can stand to look. He positions himself in front of me, trying to prevent me from passing by him. His serious glare is an attempt at intimidating me, but he forgets I have no reason to fear him.

I stop to face him and match his fierce stare, only to have him shift his look instantly. I hate this part of him. The caring and concerned Maverick has made his appearance. This is so much worse than his ruthless, driven personality. Ruthless I can handle; it's all this emotional shit that is making me irritated as fuck.

"I'm here for you," he continues to talk as I walk past him, even though he only allowed me enough room so I have to shoulder check him as I pass. "I owe you my fucking life. Shit, I owe you for so much more. So you'll have to learn to deal with me helping you through this, brother, because I'm not going anywhere." He moves in front of me as I turn around. I don't respond, smile, or blink, and I definitely don't fucking breathe until he finally takes a step back and gives me a foot of space. Anger is all I know anymore. I'm not even sure how I would respond to anything else, especially someone trying to help me when I don't fucking want it.

"I won't give up on you. Jade wouldn't let me if I tried. So we both know that shit means you're stuck with me." He draws in a long inhale, and I can tell he's still grasping for the perfect thing to say to fix me. He has to know by now there aren't any words with that much healing power. He finally gives up, then grips my shoulder and leaves the room.

I catch a glimpse of myself in the mirror above the dresser as I glance toward the door. *I look like shit.*

Good, because looking the way I feel makes me realize I really don't care if my life has fallen apart. The dark circles under my eyes and the two-week scruff on my face only add to the horror of the reality of what's going on inside of me. The turmoil, chaos, and constant swirling of a violent thunderstorm that's been going on for weeks, months. I'm drowning, waiting for the day for it to pull me under for good. The thing is, all of them out there in that office care about me when I sure the hell don't. But fuck it all if I want to deal with taking that first step to show I do.

Opening the door to the bedroom I've been staying in feels weird and foreign. It's not like I haven't stepped out to eat or drink; it's the fact I'm stepping out not knowing what the hell I'll find out here. The silence allows me to move forward knowing Jade isn't in the kitchen or on the couch ready to pounce, cry, or try to talk to me. I can't deal with anymore of her sessions to save me from myself.

I've been at the compound for weeks. At first I thought it would be the perfect place to come and try to get back to work, but now I'm not too sure that I haven't made a huge mistake. I know my mind isn't right to go back on duty, even though my shoulder is finally ready. The fucker is still stiff, but at least I'm back to lifting real weights again instead of the tiny barbells my physical therapist had me using. I swear to God every time I lifted my arms, I was more conscientious over the things flying out of my hand and going through the ceiling than I was over healing my shoulder.

Stepping out into the open living room, I watch Maverick out of the long window until he enters the main house of the compound, where he lives. It was great of Jade to push for me to use this back house that's reserved for guests, but I can't help but feel I'm not where I should be. The problem is, I don't know where I'm supposed to be, because no matter where I go, I won't be where I want to be.

Just as I reach for my shoes, I hear a noise behind me. I turn and inspect the room, finding it empty. But I can feel that something is off. Someone is in this house, and I sure as hell didn't let anyone in. The guys know better than to surprise me, and so does Jade, so I know it's not any of them. Who the hell would just come in unannounced?

Paranoia begins to set in, so I hurry to my room, grab my pistol, and begin scanning the house quietly for anything out of place. I can feel my heart racing as the feeling of adrenaline rushing through my veins pulls me back to the past. All of my senses are on full alert as I work to calm myself enough to go through this shit again.

Holding my gun with both hands, I make a sharp corner and glance down the hallway. I hear another bang and begin to move faster down the hall. Placing my ear next to the flat wooden surface of what should be an empty bedroom, I hear the sound of the floor creaking behind the door. *Someone is fucking in there.*

With me standing in the hall, they are blocked from escaping, left with only two options: go out of a window or come through me. Even though this is a two-story building, they would be better off taking the window option.

I'm not waiting around for whoever it is. I lift my foot and kick the door in. Instantly, I'm being screamed at by a woman without any clothes on while she attempts to cover herself without any luck. I keep my gun drawn and watch her go from covering her tits to trying to cover what's between her legs.

"What the fuck? Put your damn gun down," she yells while she begins to glare at me. One dainty hand barely covers her breasts as she attempts to hold them in place, while the other one is splayed over her crossed legs, just barely covering the necessities.

Not interested in what you have, sweetheart.

"Who are you?" My voice is loud, and I still haven't moved the gun from aiming at her head.

"I swear to God if you don't put that gun down, I'll tell my brother to kick your ass. Or better yet, I'll tell Jade to." *What the fuck, her brother?* I start to lower my hands as the realization of who she is hits me. She's Kaleb's sister.

"Why are you in here?" I give her my back and have the decency to hide my eyes from seeing her. Honestly, I don't want to see another woman. Mallory is the only one I want to see naked.

"My brother told me to stay in here until he gets the other house done. I can't stand listening to those two moan at each other every night. I heard Kaleb tell you I'm staying in here last night." She sounds frustrated, and I can hear her rustling around putting clothes on as she talks to me.

I don't remember him telling me anyone would be staying in the house with me, but honestly, I haven't been listening to anyone for weeks.

Damn. I don't want her here. Being around Jade is bad enough. Now there's another woman who'll be up my ass and in my way trying to fucking talk to me.

Fuck me. There isn't a thing I can say or do about it. This isn't my place, and I'm sure as hell not going to stake claim on it and move in here permanently.

"Just stay out of my way," I growl to her as I walk back to my room. This will be more of a reason for me to stay in my room and shut off the world. She can stay here, hell, I'll never see her with the schedule I've had lately. Sleep, piss, sleep. Sleeping my life away seems to be the only way I can get through the day since Mallory left me.

I slam my bedroom door, toss my gun on the bed, and make my way into the bathroom. My entire body aches from not moving in days. Stripping out of my clothes, I step into the shower and turn the water to as hot as it will go. I feel numb just like I do every day. Taking a hot shower is my way of feeling at least the hot water scald me.

Why would he put her in this house? He knows I'm not in the mood to deal with anyone. I can't promise to be pleasant and honestly don't give a fuck if she hates me when I scowl at her.

"Son of a bitch," I hiss out when the sting of the hot water hits my back. This is all fucked up. No matter what I do, my mind won't slow the fuck down and just let me think. I stand here trying to relieve some stress and let the frustration out, but instead, it's only growing. I lean my arms up against the tile and drop my head, letting the water run over my face. My emotions are starting to surface even though I'm trying like hell to keep them deep inside.

"Fuck." I'm so damn tired, even though I've done nothing but sleep my life away. It's not like I've had any form of solid rest in the past six months. My mind won't allow it.

I need to get my shit together so I can give Maverick and the guys the help they need, but it just seems impossible. I don't know why he's so hell bent to get me around the table. We all know that isn't a good idea. I'm not going to be of help to anyone in my current state. I'm honestly not sure I'll ever be ready to go back to all of that. It would go one of two ways: I'd either be a psycho ready to kill anything that moved, or I'd miss something huge because I can't get a motherfucking grip on reality.

I know one thing for sure: today, I need to drink. It's been exactly six months to the day since she disappeared from my life. I'm not sure how it can seem like yesterday, yet seem like a lifetime ago at the same time.

I quickly soap up, rinse off, and step out to dry off. It takes less than two minutes to finish my routine. It doesn't take long to get dressed and walk out without doing a single other thing besides putting on deodorant and brushing my teeth.

I step out of my room hoping to bypass his sister and try to feel a sense of relief that I'm going to actually go for a run today. This is me moving forward, even if it's only one step at a time. I'm slammed in the face with the smell of coffee the second I enter the kitchen. Jade and Kaleb's sister both look at me like I'm some sort of wild animal about to attack, and I'm not too sure my appearance isn't exactly that. I run my fingers through my long hair as I walk toward them both.

"I suppose he sent you over to drag my ass out of here?" Both of them flinch from the tight little huddle they were in as I enter the kitchen and head straight for the Jack I left in the cupboard.

"No. I didn't come to see you; I came to welcome Emmy." Jade slings the rudeness right back at me. I deserve it. She's been more than patient with me, but I can't let her think she can actually fix me. I'm shattered beyond repair.

And Emmy? Nice to know that's what her name is.

"I'd be more than happy to leave. She can have the place to herself." I take the bottle out of the cupboard and turn to leave. The second I've spun around to face them, Jade snatches the bottle out of my hand and meets me face-to-face.

"Hell, no. You will not start to go there with this. You need something to help ease the pain, then let's do this like we used to. Fight my ass. Just you and me, like we used to in training." I laugh at her ridiculous suggestion. She doesn't want to get into a fight with me right now. I have too much aggression and hatred for life to meet someone in a ring. I know my strength, and I won't take it out on Jade, no matter how many times she asks for it. The need to kill someone runs so deep inside of me, it's dripping into the marrow of my

bones. Jade knows better than to get the hell in my way.
We've been down this road a few too many times since I
moved here, yet she doesn't seem to give up.

"You and I are not a good match in the ring right now,
Jade, and you know it. Give me the fucking bottle and get the
hell out of my face." *Screw this.* I yank the bottle from her
hands, cross the kitchen, and not once acknowledge Kaleb's
sister. If she has the guts to stay here, then this is what she's
going to get. A prick and a man whose life is too damn
complicated to comprehend.

~~~~~

I have no idea how long I've been stretched out on this
bed. What I do know is, my mind and body are still not
numb. The lids on my heavy eyes are struggling to stay open,
and my bottle is half empty. I fight the demons inside of my
fucked-up head from pulling me under and ending me in my
sleep. Every time I close my eyes, all I see is her. Her long
hair blowing in the wind and her eyes as bright as anything I've
ever seen. The tempting smile on her gorgeous face as she
made her way to me with that sexy small bump I could never
get enough of. God, I craved her like no other before I found
out she was carrying my child, and now I struggle daily with
the memories of what it was like to be near her. *What I would
give to see her today.*

"Son of a bitch." I take one last swig and place the bottle
on the dresser. The booze is catching up to me. I'm not a big
drinker, but today I fucking need it. I pray like hell when I lay

my head on the pillow and drift so that my mind goes blank. I want my dreams to be just as empty as the hollow man I've become.

"Come here, now." Mallory has an eager, almost greedy look on her face when she walks through the door after a long day at work. Her hair is streaming wild all over the place. Obviously, she had the top down on my old '69 Mustang. Fuck. I want to grip all that wild hair in my hands and fuck her hard with my cock while my tongue consumes her perfect little mouth.

"It smells clean and fresh in here. Someone's been busy today." She saunters her sexy ass to me, and I grab her by the waist and haul her onto my lap.

"You tend to leave shit all over the place. I can't meet your parents with your panties shoved in between the cushions of the couch or my boxers on the floor because you can't keep your hands off me. So, yeah, I cleaned the house. How was your day?" I'm concerned about how sick she's been lately. She has the worst case of morning sickness I've ever heard of. Of course, I haven't had any experience at all around a pregnant woman, but shit, Mallory is constantly throwing up or dry heaving. The doctor told us it was normal, but fuck, I still hate seeing her with her head over the toilet while I'm holding her hair out of the way. That is not how I envision my hands in her hair.

"Much better today, and you?" She wiggles her sexy ass over my raging cock, and I lift a brow in warning before I answer.

"It was good. I'm sick of shuffling papers around on a goddamn desk though. I can't wait to get back to what I was born to do." She frowns, because we both know the day is coming soon where I'll be given the clear to be able to return to active duty. With me being shot in the shoulder almost a year ago trying to help save my best friend, Jade's, life, I've been taken off active duty, and now, well, the time has come for me to hopefully get the all clear from my commanding officer to get my ass back out there. I'm one of the best interpreters they have.

It's a craving we all have when you're trained to kill the enemy. The electric calm before the storm. Your body beyond the level of agitation and determination to get to the end result of the mission. I crave the interrogation after the capture most of all. There's nothing like watching them squirm and practically beg for their life after they refuse for hours, or even days. I have a way with breaking them. All you have to do is get them where it hurts.

I can feel it in my blood now. That sweet smell of fear as they act like they're innocent and I'm the guilty scum of the earth. They know they're going to die, and still they'll spit in my face, call me names until I have no choice but to either pull the trigger or make them suffer a long, slow, torturous death. It's not my call. It's a mission. I just do my job.

"Hey, where did that mind of yours go? You still worried about your physical therapist turning her report in?" Mallory places her hands across my clean-shaven face and then tilts my head back so I'm looking into those deep green eyes of hers. I've fallen hard for this incredible woman who before we know it will be holding our child in her arms. She's so fucking beautiful. I can't wait to hear the baby's heartbeat next week and watch her belly grow for as long as I get to before I leave.

"Nah. What I have on my mind has nothing to do with work; it has everything to do with you and the precious human you have growing inside of you." I grip ahold of her ass, tugging her over my throbbing dick, causing it to twitch with the anticipation of what's to come.

"God, Beau," she moans into my neck. "What am I going to do with you?"

A half hour later, she's ridden my cock, screamed my name, and is now in the bathroom cleaning herself up before her parents get here. I'm still in the same spot on the couch praying like a motherfucker that for once in my life when our child comes into this world I'm here to witness it. I want to watch him or her take their first breath and not be out on some mission across the world. Being in the Special Forces has always been my dream, and I made it a reality, but now I can't help but feel that ping of guilt that I'll miss important moments in my child's life.

"Goddamn it." I wake, jolting upright in bed and tweaking the hell out of my shoulder. "Son of a bitch." *Why? Why in God's name do I keep torturing myself with nightmares and memories that will never be?*

Everywhere I look, she's there. Every damn time I close my eyes, she's there. I can't get away from her no matter what I do or how hard I try. Even a bottle of booze won't drown out the fact she fucking left me.

I swing my legs around the side of the bed and sit there in pure defeat. My head is killing me, and my body is drained from the way I've done nothing good to it in months. I need to get the hell out of here before I completely lose my mind.

A quick glance at the clock lets me know I've at least gotten through half of another day. I grumble at the thought of that shit. One day seems to bleed right into the next right now. It won't be long until I won't have a life at all, which is fine by me.

The muscles in my neck start to twitch, and the pain begins to travel its way down my arms until it hits the tips of my fingers. I lay my elbows on my knees and drop my head into my palms to try to control my temper. I want to beat the shit out of something and not stop until my body can't move another muscle. I need to take out all of this anger, and I need to do it now.

I lift my head to look around the room that's been my escape for the past several weeks. The sheets on the bed need changed, my clothes are piled up in every corner, and there are water bottles all over the room. Yeah, this is the way to fucking live, right here, cooped up in a room in the middle of a security detailed compound because your friends are worried about you.

"Fuck it all." I reach for my running shoes and quickly shove them on. I'm not in the mood to run, but this pent-up anger needs to be taken out on something, and I sure as hell won't agree to take it out on Jade even though fighting is exactly what I need.

What I need is to hit someone else. Someone who won't talk back but will taunt me nonetheless. He's been provoking me for days and practically begging me to get in the ring with him as well. Maybe it's time I take him up on that.

He wants me to let it all out on him. Well, today's that day. "I hope you're ready for me, Kaleb."

CHAPTER TWO

HARRIS

There's no one around when I enter the kitchen. *Thank fuck.* Hopefully, Jade realized I'm in no shape to have anyone staying in this house with me, especially a woman. She's nothing like the woman I want here with me anyway. In fact, they're complete opposites. Mallory's tall stature made her curves look like they went on for miles, her tits fit perfectly in my hands, and her ass was made to be grabbed. Her blonde hair felt like silk when I would wrap it around my hands and yank it back to attack that long, smooth neck of hers. The only thing I noticed about this chick was her hair is as black as my heart and as dark as I feel. I pray to God she's gone soon, because I don't need to look at all that hair to remind me that my life is nothing but a black fucking hole.

"You need to stop," I say to myself quietly, then pick up my phone and shoot Kaleb a text telling him to meet me in the gym. I turn to grab a bottle of water out of the fridge while I wait for him to reply, and that's when I notice *her.* Out of the corner of my eye, I see his sister outside the kitchen window with a big motherfucking revolver in her hands. I sure the hell hope she knows what she's doing with that beast.

"Fuck me," I whisper when I see the type of gun she has. A .357 Magnum. Those bitches can shoot the length of a few football fields in a second, and it will knock her on her ass and dislocate her arm from her shoulder if she's out there fucking around. Her stance seems perfect, her body relaxed, and she's completely focused on something through the sight of the gun.

It pisses me off that I'm intrigued. That woman I saw earlier does not strike me as some sharp-shooting pistol expert. Although, I must say now while I inspect her from head to toe, she's toned and firm. And to top it off, she is Kaleb's sister. He probably taught her how to shoot the thing.

If I had a sister, I would've done the same damn thing. Can't blame the man after the shit that went down with their brother. But damn, that is one wicked weapon.

I watch her for mere seconds before my phone vibrates on the counter. I pull my eyes away from her and retrieve my phone, knowing it's Kaleb and thanking his goddamn ass for saving me from watching this distraction I do not want or need. I slide the screen and respond to Kaleb that I'll meet him in five minutes.

My eyes can't help but divert back to her. I watch her bend down and gather all her stuff before she starts heading back this way. Not once did I hear that powerful gun go off. Someone needs to tell her that little girls shouldn't play with a gun like that, for fuck's sake. She's more than likely bored out of her mind back here where we're secluded, so she's looking for something to kill some time.

I'm in no mood to strike up a conversation or pretend to be a nice guy with a woman I want nothing to do with, so I grab my water and leave the house. The conversation I have in mind has to do with my goddamn fists and not with the sister of the man's ass I'm about to kick.

I run to the gym that's attached to the main house. This is one area the guys didn't skimp on, and I need to appreciate it more than I have.

I hit the door and feel relief when I see Kaleb. "You sure you're up to getting the shit beaten out of you?" The heated tone in his voice and the smirk he has on his face piss me off even more when I walk into the gym. Kaleb's standing in the middle of the ring already with no gloves on. Seeing him ready to throw down pumps the much-needed adrenaline I need and excites me more than I expected. This is the shit I need to feel alive again.

"Fuck you too." I toss the water bottle on the floor beside the ring, climb the couple of steps up, and dip my body down to enter through the ropes. I'm weak as fuck, and he can smell it. The way he's glaring at me with some self-satisfied smirk on his face and his stance ready to pounce only pisses me off more. I may look and feel like shit, but the things he's gone through are nothing compared to the war that's waiting to be fought inside of my head. He has his woman. She didn't leave him and vanish right before his eyes, leaving his world to crumble, his heart to collapse, and his goddamn mind to disappear with her.

"You going to stand there all day or get this shit done and over with, bitch?" He stands with his arms spread open as if he's waiting for me to drive the first punch. That's exactly what I do. I nail him with a right hook that lands on the side of his temple. He staggers, but before I have time to swing again, he plows into me with a kick to my stomach, followed by a punch that leads to a crunching noise from my nose. Blood spurts down my face, and pain ricochets from one side of my head to the other. His arms go up like he's challenging me to come at him again.

"Come on, Harris, you need this. I can take it, you pussy. Let's go." And I explode with that phrase. I grab him by the back of the neck, rolling us to the floor. Fists start flying fast and furious as if we're fighting for our lives. An explosive punch to his ribs sets him off exactly how I want him. He attacks with the force I need. Brutal punches to my face bring pain to the surface before a sweep of my leg has me dropping back down to the floor. I welcome the pain. I need the pain. It eggs me on and revitalizes me in a way I crave.

My next move is both spontaneous and unpredictable even to myself. I move swiftly and smoothly, snapping up off the floor. A swift kick to his jaw before I tumble backwards leaves him stunned and holding his face.

This is a fight with no rules, no winner, where neither one of us is looking to be the undisclosed master. It's a language all of its own. This is a lesson I need and one he's been dying to give. Only, I don't plan to make it easy on him.

I know I'm hiding behind a mask of despair, and knowing this is when I let my guard down, when I decide to surrender and allow the man who has been doing his job as a friend to try and bring me back to the man I once was. I allow him to get one last destructive punch in. This is the one I need the most. The one that clearly knocks me on my goddamn ass until I'm lying there breathing heavily.

My mind starts to tell me it's time to move on. My chest explodes inside, and I finally feel the shards of reality that are heating up the blood pumping through my veins. It's time to realize she isn't coming back to me. It's time for me to take the lesson of life that has pulled me under this rough, intense current of self-destruction. It's his punch to the side of my head that fucking makes me feel I'm alive. Here's the best part though, I don't care if I'm alive. I care about nothing. This isn't living, and yet it's all I've got.

"What the hell is going on in here?" I squeeze my eyes shut, not from the pain or the fact that blood is dripping out of my nose and my busted up lip; it's the tone of a very pissed-off Jade that has me shutting out the world.

I open my eyes and peer up at Kaleb standing there with his hand stretched out, his chest rising and falling, a nice shiner already forming around his left eye, and what appears to be a gash on his right cheek. He's pressing a hand to his right side, and I can tell he's hurting.

Pain. All I feel is pain. The physical sense of it I can live with. I want more of it. If only to knock me the hell out for days, weeks at a time to make the excruciating discomfort inside my chest disappear.

"You feel better now?" Kaleb asks, and for a split second, I want to smile as he glances down at me with a shit-eating grin on his face. Fuck, I have no idea when I last smiled. I do, actually, but I sure as hell won't allow my mind to go there. I take hold of his hand, allowing him to pull me up.

"I feel about as bad as you look, motherfucker." I turn and spit out the blood that's been filling my mouth.

"Good. Then my job here is done. Get yourself cleaned up. Have some dinner. Get some strength back, because Jade can punch harder than you." I growl at his comment, ready to tell him to go look at his face then tell me that when the sound coming from Jade has me closing my mouth.

"By the looks of it, I should beat both of your asses. Is this what you think you need, Harris? For the two of you idiots to beat on each other? This is not what I meant when I asked you to fight with me. I wanted to get your blood flowing back in your system, to give your body a workout, pump up the adrenaline. Jesus, this is crazy. This only proves to me you need help. God, what's gotten into the two of you?" I say nothing. It's none of her business what the hell I do or how I go about doing it.

If this is the way I want to work through my shit in my head, then it's my decision, not hers. She may have been trained the same way as the rest of us, but the underlying fact here is she is a woman. She doesn't understand that inflicting pain on yourself and others in a physical way is what a man as fucked up as I am needs.

"Settle the hell down, Jade." Kaleb snags her around the waist, pulling her close to him. I feel it again. That painful, jealous rage that wants to claw its way to my soul and drive, twist that bolt of envy whenever I see the two of them together hitting me hard. I wince from the way he holds her tight, which has Jade rushing to my side to inspect my injuries. She's always telling me with each passing day that my battered heart will heal. What the hell do any of them know anyway? These two have each other. My entire world has left me.

"I'm fine," I tell her, backing away before she reaches up to inspect my face like the mother hen she's been lately.

"Are you now? The two of you beating on each other like you hate one another makes you fine? This isn't healthy. You smell like booze; you look like hell. Please stop doing this to yourself. I need my best friend back. I miss you," she pleas with sadness in her eyes. I have to look away.

"Thanks for this. I needed it." I lift my chin at Kaleb. I can't handle Jade right now. I know she's hurting like I am. It's not until my hands grip the handle on the door that I feel like an asshole for not responding to her. I'm not going to give her some fucked-up excuse, lie to her, and admit she'll get me back as a friend. How can I be a friend when I am barely breathing through each day? Why would I want to come back? I have nothing to return to.

I keep my back to the two of them, shove open the door, and say, "You bring me back my light, and you'll get your friend back. Until then, leave me in the fucking dark."

I'm almost to my cabin when I hear footsteps rushing up behind me. "You asshole. Don't you think I fucking miss her too?" Jade punches me in the chest, knocking the wind from me the second I turn around. "Don't you think I want to ball up in a hole and die because of what happened? I'm fucking gutted and trying to grieve, and your selfish ass refuses to even exist. Well, guess what, she was in your life for months…She was in mine for years. How am I supposed to remember to live when I have to keep reminding you to fucking get out of bed? If you're so fucking miserable here, then take your ass somewhere else." Her words echo in my ears, and I can finally feel someone else's emotions for the first time since I held Mallory's lifeless body in my arms.

"I loved her. I know you were happy with her, and I wish like hell I could bring her back to you, even if it's for one last laugh. She would've been a great mom." And with that, she bursts into tears, causing my heart to sink deeper into the darkness.

I can't process what to say to her, because I'm too numb to respond. The only response I have is to wrap my arms around her when she steps close to me and fight back my own tears as she cries into my chest.

I wish it had been me who died that day.

CHAPTER THREE

EMMY

That man is a walking time bomb. He walks around here like an arrogant jerk. I would rather sleep outside and let the bugs eat away at me than stay in this house with him, but I won't; and knowing how protective Kaleb is of me, he wouldn't allow it anyway.

Kaleb's protection is what has me here in the first place.

"None of us are safe, Sis. You and mom are coming to the compound where I know I can protect you. End of fucking story. Go pack your shit now." That's all we got. No reason why we're here. No explanation. Not a damn thing. We made him let me finish my semester out and he only allowed that with extra security on us at all times.

I'm in my third year of medical school, and I'm royally screwed. I'm not allowed on the computer, no communication with anyone back home. Not that I had time to associate with anyone outside of school when I was in Florida. My school life is extremely hectic. All I've ever wanted was to practice medicine and become a doctor. And now because of a threat that I'm being left in the dark about, I'm fucked.

Guilt hits me, and I slump down in the kitchen chair farther as I sit here in this stunning house with top-of-the-line stainless steel appliances in my vision. Smooth earth-toned countertops and a view that steals my breath away. I stare out of the window at the different colors of green along the plateau and ridges overlooking this particular beautiful region of our country and try to stomach the awkward position I'm in.

I met Beau briefly about six months ago. I remember it well. However, the way he looked at me earlier tells me he doesn't recall meeting me at all. I can't say I blame him, really; the man has been through hell. The hollow look in his eyes tells me he's still living in the depths of it. Not to mention everything that Jade has told me about the way he recluses himself in that room. He barely eats and refuses to talk to anyone. His situation is what has me feeling like a bitch for wanting to tear into his ass for being such an asshole.

You would think after growing up with a man like my brother that I would be used to men ordering me around, but I'm not. Kaleb I can handle. The two of us are as close as siblings should be. Especially after everything my family has been through with our brother, Ty. His drugs and verbal abuse toward my mother were more than I could handle.

Then his sudden disappearance years ago, when we all actually thought he was dead, didn't make it any better. Only, he was very much alive, living in Mexico as a drug lord, running a traffic operation, the illegal life completely consuming his life in a way I can't begin to fathom.

His connections in the cartel eventually led Kaleb directly to him. Unfortunately, when Kaleb was captured, Ty tortured him as if he were the enemy instead of the brother who tried to help him before he disappeared. And God...he would have killed the only brother I've truly had if it hadn't been for Jade and the rest of the guys finding him and saving his life. I really believe Ty would have killed Kaleb.

It tore my mother's heart out of her chest. She's still grieving the loss of her son to this day. While as screwed up as it is, I'm not. I lost my brother, Ty, years ago. His death hurt me, but not in the way it has my mother, because I mourned the loss years ago when he became an evil shell of himself with no morals.

My mind drifts back to Beau and the fact behind the reason he's living the worst nightmare any person could live. The not knowing and the tragedy of a loss that great saddens me. I've been kept in the dark about all of the details, but I don't have to know anything to know he's gutted and has lost his will to exist the way he used to.

For whatever reason, Beau hates me. I can sense it even when he's not in the house. The minute those deep blue eyes of his met mine this morning, I could tell he despised me. I may go to hell though, because even knowing about the depth of his pain, it didn't stop me from looking at his tight ass when he turned around. Or that massive, thick chest, those strong legs, and...God, I need to stop. This isn't right. I'm mentally mind fucking a man who doesn't know I exist. And for God's sake, he shouldn't either, especially after he lost his fiancée and baby like that.

I need to do something, anything to take my mind off him. I sit upright, slide my body out of the chair, and jump, clutching my hand to my chest when I see Beau standing in the doorway. His face is covered in blood and sweat. His eyes stare at me like he wants to shoot me dead. He's gripping his side too. The man is hurt, and I don't know if I should offer my help or let him be. My mouth processes the decision for me when the words seem to tumble out unexpectedly.

"What happened to you?" I ask while trying to remain calm and willing my feet not to go to him and help him like he truly needs. It's only a few seconds before my healing instincts kick in and I start to walk toward him. He looks like he's had the shit beat out of him, and I can't just let him bleed.

"Nothing." He takes a few steps toward the kitchen and turns on the water when I finally give in to the instinct taking over.

"You may need stitches." I walk toward him, quickly pulling out a few towels along the way.

"I don't need any damn stitches. I'm fine." He's irritated, but in this moment, I don't let him intimidate me. I need to see for myself just how deep these cuts go.

"Who did this to you?" He tenses up when I touch his arm, but I step in beside him so I can see just how bad that one on his right eye is.

"I did it to myself." As soon as my finger touches his face, he pulls away from me. My eye follows the blood trickling down to his chest as it continues to stain his shirt.

"You may as well get over yourself. I'm going to check on that one cut before this conversation is over, so you can do

us both a favor and stand still long enough for me to see it."
He takes a deep breath and stands against the cabinet in his
pissed-off demeanor. "Let me clean it up so I can see it
better."

"Just hurry the hell up. I need a shower." His eyes are
dark, and so far, there's not too much swelling.

"If you don't put ice on this, the swelling will get worse."
I'm worried about who did this to him. Do I need to call Kaleb
and make sure he knows this guy was attacked?

He lets me get closer, but I can feel he's one word from
bolting, so I stop talking. I wipe the blood off his cheek and
exhale with relief when I see the blood makes it look worse
than it truly is. I just find it sad to see his gorgeous face
marked in any way.

It's hard to breathe this close to him. I can feel hurt and
anger radiating from his entire body and can't help but feel a
deep sadness when I look into his face. If I didn't know what
his response would be, I'd ask him what it was that truly hurt
him.

"It looks like you'll be fine, but I'd like you to let me put
something on it when you get out of the shower." He watches
me closely as I continue to inspect his face and neck. I keep a
professional outlook on this even though he's no doubt one of
the sexiest men I've ever seen in my life.

He's hurt so much deeper than these minor cuts and
bruises. I can feel it. I take a step back knowing he's reached
his limit of me fussing over his wounds. He finally takes a

breath and walks away as soon as I give him the space to move.

I'm not going to pry, however, I'm going to hope. Hope that somehow the man I can tell is dying inside can turn his life around and be the kind, caring and yet hard-ass man Jade has told me so much about. Beau Harris is in there somewhere; I hope he figures out how to make it through the darkness.

CHAPTER FOUR

HARRIS

Fuck. I should've never let her close enough to touch me. I can still smell her as I make my way into the bathroom, slamming the door shut behind me. For one minute, her smell intoxicated me, a minute that was way too long for my liking. Her touch wasn't supposed to make me feel anything, yet it did. She feels like sin, and that's the last thing I need to get mixed up in. Her sassy personality and her body are a dangerous combination and something I need to stay the fuck away from. Besides that, I don't know a damn thing about her except she's Kaleb's sister. *What in the ever loving fuck is wrong with me?*

Her eyes were so focused on cleaning me up, but I couldn't help but notice them. She was so intense as she inspected me through the bluest eyes I've ever seen. She held me captive without even looking to meet my eyes. She would hate me more than I believe she already does if she had. I'm empty, hollow, and I have nothing but anger to see. She didn't tell me what she did for a living, but by the way her sturdy hands inspected my face, she has to be in the medical field.

The way she stormed right over to me and bossed me around proves she isn't afraid of me one bit. That alone should piss me off, but I guess I shouldn't expect anything less from a Maverick. I mean, look who her brother is. *For fuck's sake, Beau, get her out of your head.*

I crack my head from side to side as if I can shake those thoughts of her out of my head, when what I'm really trying to do is shake the unnerving feeling she's creating in me. I shouldn't be feeling a fucking thing at all, and that woman out there knows it. I wonder if she knows how dark I am and how screwed up my mind is? If she did, she would run as far away from me as she could.

I need her gone so I can escape back to my introverted ways. *Alone.* I'm done talking to her. It wouldn't surprise me one bit if she were here on Jade's request. That stubborn woman will do anything to save me. Bringing a woman here is not going to bring back the friend she lost. That man is gone forever.

I know Jade's hurting as much as I am. Christ, I've never seen her lose it like she did at Mallory's funeral. Not even when she thought she would never see Kaleb again. But then again, with him, there was hope. With my woman and my child, there was nothing. Only a coffin that held my soul in it. My life. My heart. My world.

I flip the lever on the shower, bend and untie my shoes, slipping them off my feet and ridding myself of these sweaty and blood-stained shorts.

The hot water burns the hell out of my face when I step in to rinse the rest of the blood away.

With my eyes tightly closed, I can see her face. Her smile. Her expression when we walked out of the doctor's office that day is something I'll never forget. Both of us were so happy after hearing our baby's heartbeat. When she first told me she was pregnant, I was shocked and terrified, which quickly turned to excitement as the reality of it all slammed me in the heart. I couldn't wait to meet our baby.

Now, the only thing I hold on to is the hope I'll come face-to-face with the person who took it all away from me.

All of it vanished that day. Blood, so much blood there wasn't a thing I could do but drop to the ground and hold her, screaming for them both to come back to me. She died instantly. I didn't even have the chance to tell her good-bye. I wanted like hell for it not to be true. Her eyes were completely vacant, while her left hand sparkled with the diamond I gave her and the dreams I had wished for us and our future family. I loved her and our unborn child, and some crazy son of a bitch took them both from me.

"Fuck!" I yell out without a worry if anyone can hear me. Why did this all happen? Why didn't they kill me instead? Who in their right mind would kill a woman, let alone a pregnant woman, and why in the hell would they snipe her of all people out?

Every goddamn report that came back proved to be the same. Mallory was murdered. She was a hit. A mark. For what, I may never know. She never hurt anyone, and I'm worried like hell that what I'll find out is the only mistake she made was fall in love with me.

I know Kaleb and all the guys are busting their asses to try and figure this out. I should be helping them. But I'm honestly afraid of what they'll find. Something tells me that it was me this person was really after and she took the bullet right between her eyes for me.

There's no way that mark was meant for her. It has to be a warning from someone trying to prove a point. Well, point fucking made, motherfucker.

No wonder Maverick moved his sister here. He's keeping her safe.

If that's the reason, then I want her safe as well, but not in this house with me. Hell, send her to stay with Jackson. That man will have her laughing from the crazy spilling out of his unfiltered mouth that never shuts up. He can talk all day long, while the last thing I want to do is talk at all.

Maverick is out of his mind if he thinks she's safe with me. Even I know this. I'm as unstable as they come. I need to talk to him. He needs to be told that either she goes, or I do. He can move her to a different house, so I don't have to worry about who I offend, which is destined to happen if she's left with me.

Fuck it. If he won't force her to move, I'll leave. I'm not sure where I'll go, but I'll find somewhere new. Every place I could go from my past will be a reminder of Mal.

Fuck. Maybe I should try to get my shit together and prove to the Army I'm stable enough to go out on missions. That'll get me the fuck out of here and away from everyone.

My stomach growls in the middle of my tormented breakdown. Go fucking figure. It has to be a sign for me to get my ass cleaned up and out of here. And I mean out of this house. Away from all of this. My head is so screwed up right now I'm surprised I'm able to stand upright.

I grab the soap and wash away the last bit of blood on my knuckles. Once I'm done cleaning the rest of my body and rinsing off, I twist the knob, shut off the water, and step out into the steam-filled room.

"Shit. No clean towels," I mumble as I open the door to the bedroom. I jerk to a complete halt when I see the room is picked up, the bed is made, and a clean towel is lying on the bed. Oh fuck no, she did not come in here and invade my space. *Who the hell does she think she is? She's another Jade, for Christ sake.*

I grab the towel and quickly dry off. I am fucking livid pissed, and at this point, I don't care if she is Kaleb's sister. She needs to stay the fuck away from my shit and the hell away from me all together for that matter.

It takes me two minutes tops to get dressed and storm out of this room. I'm a man out to prove a point to a woman who has no idea the kind of shit storm she has just created inside of me.

"What the fuck do you think you're doing?" I hiss at her when I see her standing in the kitchen preparing food. She's fucking cooking? In a dress that shows off every curve of a body that is pure woman? I clench my hands, digging them hard into the skin on my palms just to see if I'm having some kind of lucid dream of an angel dressed in white standing in front of me.

"I'm going to pretend you didn't just yell at me like that and ignore the fact you're looking at me with that much disgust. Instead, I'm going to say you're welcome." She's calm. Calm enough that it pisses me off even more. The minute the words tumble out of my mouth, I instantly regret saying them, but maybe this time she will listen.

"You need to stay the fuck away from me. I don't want you here. I don't need you here. And I sure as hell don't like you here."

"I wanted to help you. To show you that you have a friend. Someone who—" I cut her off with a lift of my hand and three steps toward her. Christ almighty, she is beautiful. This is the first time I'm truly paying attention to the way she looks.

Her hair. I have never seen a woman with as much hair as she has. It's long, shiny, and fits her in a way I can't explain. She's simply beautiful, and the fact I'm even noticing that pisses me off.

"I don't need a friend." My glare into her eyes allows me to see how my words hit her. She immediately looks down and takes a deep breath just before the front door flies open. I close my eyes, wanting to kill whoever that is. I've seen three people too many today. This one may be the one to do me in.

"Good, you're making food. We're going to need some of that." Jackson moves straight for Emmy and places a kiss in her hair as he puts his arm around her. Kaleb and the rest of the guys begin to file in one at a time, allowing Jade to be the last through the door. Her weary eyes catch mine, and I immediately turn away from her.

Ten minutes ago, all I wanted was to be left alone, and now that everyone is strolling on in here like they're ready to get shit faced, I realize it's actually the first time in months I've felt like hanging out. It's a much better alternative to being left alone in this house with Emmy and the seriousness that surrounds me. It's kind of crazy when a minute ago I wanted to choke anyone who came near me, yet all of a sudden, I'm seeing how the distraction is exactly what I need.

"It's fucking party time, motherfucker. We need some bro time, and your ass needs to fucking smile a time or two before we leave here." Jackson leaves Emmy and walks straight over to me with a bottle of beer. His smile and that damn southern drawl pulls at my anger inside and honestly begins to make me feel better with his easy laughter about everything.

"Do you always laugh, Jackson? Shit, guys, how much alcohol did you bring?" Emmy calls out from behind me over the chatter of the rest of the guys and the sounds of bottles clanking on the bar as they all set down what they carried in.

"Not enough, darling, and yes, pretty thing, I do," he answers both her questions and pulls her in tight for a hug from behind. He's laughing and flirting with her for a few seconds, and I can see his playful personality lighting up everyone in the room, except for me. Emmy pauses to look at me during all the chaos, and I can see her face change from a bright smile to unhappy instantaneously. I regret my attack on her right before they walked in the door and now wish like fuck I could get my shit together and stop the constant destruction I cause when it comes to everyone who crosses into my path anymore.

"Who needs a shot of tequila? Pierce bought the good shit!" Steele starts pouring shots, and I still haven't moved a muscle. I know these guys all mean well, but shit, the more I think about it, the more I decide that this is a bad idea.

"Stone, get over here. You're first, because I can feel you need to lighten the fuck up over there." Steele holds a large shot glass in the air. I finally say fuck it and take a step toward the party. Hell, if nothing else, I'll be able to lighten up a little, and who knows, if I dip into this tequila they claim is the good shit, then maybe I'll forget for one night and sleep without nightmares.

Stone. I haven't been called that in months. The Army called me Harris. Stone is my call name from when I went on missions with the Elite Forces group Kaleb Maverick owns. His call name is Fire, and of course, he named Jade Ice to compliment his own name. Those two are fucking perfect for each other. I look over and see the two of them in each other's arms as they look at me. I know they just want to see me pull through this heartache, but right now, I just need some fucking time.

"Alright. I'm grilling burgers. Who wants some?" Emmy starts talking over everyone as Jade reaches to hand her several packages of hamburger meat.

"Just cook everything you have. We're gonna be here awhile, Sis," Maverick calls out to her. I make it a personal mission to lighten the hell up tonight, especially if all of my friends are willing to spend the evening with my cranky ass.

"Alright, let's do this shit." Jackson's voice is deeper than normal as he steps up beside me and all the guys grab a shot glass. "Does someone have some special toast before we start this shit show?" We all look around and end at Jackson. I've been around these guys enough to know this is right up his alley.

"To Stone making it to the ring today. Even though I heard Kaleb kicked his ass." Jade turns and half smiles at him before he continues. The asshole smirks like he won some damn medal or some shit. He looks as roughed up as I do. A nice damn shiner to go along with that cocky grin on his arrogant face. "And to all of you motherfuckers. For being like brothers and never leaving a man down. Tonight, we drink, and tomorrow, we sleep, because something tells me this is going to be one hell of a fucking drink fest." He holds up his glass, and we all follow.

The tequila is smooth. I hardly feel a burn as it goes down my throat. "That's good shit. I fucking love ya, Steele." Jackson's loud voice erupts just as I set my shot glass on the table, causing me to laugh.

"Gran Patròn, brother. The smoothest out there. Guaranteed to knock you on your goddamn ass if you flirt with it too long." Steele's smooth talking matches the calmness in his personality as he takes the bottle and begins to pour another round. Holy shit, these guys are not kidding around tonight, and to be honest, it's something I'm now looking forward to.

CHAPTER FIVE

HARRIS

I feel fucking amazing kicked back in a chair on the deck as the night air brushes over my face. The sound of everyone laughing and joking has made my night, and to be honest, it's obvious this is something I really needed.

Pierce and Kaleb talked to me briefly about getting my ass to the table on Monday, come hell or high water, so I know that's going to be inevitable.

There's a small part of me that dreads it, but I know I need them. I need this in my life again.

"Alright, who made the fucking rules about not bringing the pussy to the compound tonight? Because they should be dick punched right now." Jackson stands in front of everyone and pushes down on his dick. "Fuck me. Why does whiskey make me horny as fuck?" He turns to Emmy with those fuck me eyes of his, and she laughs while shaking her head no to him. "I'm messing with ya, woman." He winks at her and puckers his lips to kiss at her.

I catch a glimpse of her dress blowing around the top part of her legs and literally lower myself in the lounge chair, trying to catch a glimpse of her ass when she turns to say something to him. Nice ass. She must feel my stare, because she pulls the dress down a few more inches. *What the fuck am I doing?*

"Who's ready for another shot?" I stand quickly as I shout to everyone before I stumble over the boots at the door and walk inside. Steele is the only one who follows, and I decide it's the last one for me the second I feel the burn go down.

"You know I'm here for you if you need anything. I'm sorry I haven't been in here to drag your ass out yet. We had strict orders to be nice to you, so I have been. Just know those orders have been lifted, so get used to my pretty face." He smiles with those pearly whites of his before he shakes my hand firmly. "I'm headed to bed. See you tomorrow."

Just as he leaves out the front door, Jade walks in followed by all the rest of them. "I'm tired, so Kaleb and I are leaving. This has been fun. I missed your smile." Jade steps into my arms and wraps her arms around my back.

"I missed it too," I say softly, hugging her back for the first time in months. I missed laughing and joking with these guys more than I'd like to admit, and even though I've pushed her away from me, I miss Jade too. Once you've been through what we've been through together, you tend to feel like they're a part of you. When they're not around, you're missing part of yourself.

"Alright, don't make me do this every night just to see it. I'll be bringing the crew in again if it comes to that. Trust me, you'll smile just to get them out of here, especially

Jackson." She pulls away with a warning look. I should've
known she orchestrated this.

"Got it, Captain." She smiles wide, and Kaleb literally
moans as he steps behind her and pulls her against his
chest.

"Fuck. Don't call her that. You'll get me all crazy
thinking about our days in the desert again." His laughter is
deep as she wraps her arms over his. I feel a pang of jealousy
as I watch their interaction. He lifts her up, hoisting her half-
drunk ass over his shoulder before he barrels through the
door. Her laughter fills the room, and everyone has no choice
but to smile at the two of them. I'm not jealous they're
together; I just miss my happiness, even if it was short lived.

"Night, guys," Pierce calls out, leading the way while
they all leave me standing in a quiet house. The back door is
open, and I realize Emmy never came in.

Guilt washes over me again as I think about how I
talked to her before they all showed up tonight. "Fuck." I know
I need to apologize. She was just trying to help me, but she
needs to know when to help and when to stay away. And that
the majority of the time, she just needs to stand clear of me,
and we'll get along just fine.

I step outside and stop in my tracks the instant I see
her. She's stretching near the steps, the landscape light
shining straight through her dress.

This time, her tits catch my attention, because I'm just
noticing she isn't wearing a bra. The curve of her breasts

shows through the white material, which is all I get to see before she notices me and steps closer. The light no longer shines through, and damn it, that irritates me. *She has perfect fucking tits.*

"Good night." Her arm brushes mine as she walks past me. Her heels make loud footsteps on the wood floor, echoing through my ears, going straight to my dick.

As much as I may regret doing this later, I can't help myself. Her fresh scent is the final straw that has me turning around and taking the steps to follow her down her hall. She stops in front of her door to look at me, confused, just before my lips smash into hers. *Fuck me.* Tequila and sin. I'm ruined. Her tongue lies flat for one fraction of a second, but when I suck it into my mouth, she groans, and that is all it takes for our kiss to turn into a frenzy.

She hesitates again, but only for a second as my hands begin to travel down her body. I pull my mouth from hers and bury my face into her neck. And. I. Inhale.

"I may hate myself for this tomorrow. But right now, I need this." I can feel her body tense up as I whisper into her ear, and it isn't until she runs her hands down my arms that I move forward.

"Do you like this dress?" Any restraint I've had is thrown out of the fucking window the more I feel her soft skin under my palms and against my lips. I have to ask her if she wants this dress, because I'm about to rip this fucking thing right off of her.

She moans a pathetic, "Mhmm," as I bite her shoulder.

"Tell me where to buy you another one." And with that, I rip it off of her. The sound of the material shredding literally lights a fire between us, and we both reach for my belt in desperation.

I don't think about anything else when I smash her against her door and lift her legs around my waist. My hands grab her ass, and I can feel lace under my fingers. Our kissing gets more intense when I grind against her. My jeans are unbuttoned but still in place as my hard-on holds them up. I can feel the denim against my bare dick, because I chose not to wear any underwear earlier in a rush to yell at her.

"You're not supposed to feel this good," I grumble against her chest as I take one of her nipples into my mouth, biting down just hard enough to make her suck in a breath before I kiss my way to the other one.

"Neither are you," she exhales as she runs her fingernails down my back, no doubt leaving her mark. Fuck all the reasons why this is a bad idea. I can only think about the one reason it is a great idea: I need this.

I reach for her doorknob and carry her to bed. I rip her panties from the sides right as I let her fall to the mattress. She reaches for my zipper and grips my dick tightly before she pulls my jeans down my legs. I reach for my jeans just as the realization hits me.

"Fuck, I don't have a condom." I haven't needed any for a very long time. I haven't had the urge to need one in months.

"I'm on the pill. Don't stop." She places her hands on mine and pulls the jeans from my grip. I give in and let her take my dick into her mouth and feel her warm, wet tongue instantly moving across the underside.

I grab a fistful of her hair when she starts to move up and down on me. My grip allows her to take me deeper as I press into her throat.

"Fuck." *She knows how to suck cock.* She swallows with the tip of my dick in her throat, and I feel my release racing to the surface. No way am I blowing my load in her mouth. I want in her pussy. The need to fuck the hell out her takes control of my mind. I'm about to lose myself as I pound this girl into the mattress until my body can no longer handle it. This is going to be pure fucking and nothing more.

"Get on all fours on the bed." She listens immediately, and I stroke my cock as I watch her spread her knees apart and look back at me over her shoulder.

"I like it rough. I'm not gentle," I try to warn her, because I know this will be rough sex for me. It's been pent up so long, and I know how I'm going to explode quickly.

"Good, because so do I, so don't hold back on me." And with that, I slam into her. My grip on her hips is tight and will leave a mark, but that's only to get her into place. I need to be deeper. Once I get all the way in after a few thrusts, I move my hands to her shoulders and begin to fuck her relentlessly. She arches her back perfectly, and I notice ink on her back, but not the details.

There's no dirty talk like I usually do. It's just friction and fucking like I truly need.

I pull her torso against my chest and slide one hand over her neck, squeezing lightly. Her reaction to it only makes me thrust faster and causes her quick release as my grip releases around her neck.

Fuck, she likes it rough, and I'm just touching the surface of what I can do, but I can't hold back any longer. Her pussy squeezes around my cock, and I'm done.

My release pours into her, and I collapse with her on the bed. My jeans are at my ankles, and my body is drenched in sweat, but I don't care about anything in the world except sleep.

~~~

I stir when I wake, my eyes adjusting to the light coming in through the windows. My head is pounding, and I'm sweating like crazy, so I'm guessing this is my punishment for the tequila last night. "Shit," I whisper when I see nothing but a mass of dark hair splayed across my bare chest. The throbbing behind my eyes proceeds to kick up about twenty notches, because I know exactly whose head of hair that is.

Every damn moment of last night is flashing through my head as I plummet down memory lane. I fucked her. Twice. *Son of a bitch.*

How the hell could I do this? It had to be the booze. There's no way in hell I would take advantage of a chick like her if I hadn't sucked down half a bottle of tequila. *Motherfucker, Maverick is going to fucking kill me.*

I stay still and stare at the hair I had pulled tight in my hands a few hours ago.

She's a greedy one; a dirty one too. I wanted her so bad last night that I took it while she gave it willingly. Now, I feel like shit. I hope like crazy she keeps this to herself. I'm not ready to face the consequences of what happened last night. Surely, she won't want her damn brother up her ass over what happened between us. I need her to keep this quiet.

I don't know what got into me. Yes, I do. It was her sweet smell that sent me into a ballistic, horny desperation. Then her soft skin ruined me. She is tight, and just thinking about that is going to corrupt the hell out of me in ways I'm not ready for if I don't get the hell out of this bed and walk away.

She stirs, and her tits rub across my chest. I force my cock to stop rousing when she blinks open her eyes. She looks up at me, and I can say I'm shocked as hell. She isn't looking at me like she expects more from me than the raw,

primal fucking we did last night. She's looking at me exactly
how I feel: guilty.

CHAPTER SIX

EMMY

We're both awake, neither one of us moving for obvious reasons. I feel like I'm suffocating to death, which leads me to believe he's struggling in ways I can't comprehend. I can feel his heart beating beneath my head frantically out of control and wish like hell I could say something to calm him down.

I don't think he's knows I'm awake; selfishly, I'm not moving. I like being in his arms even if it's the only time he'll hold me. I miss having someone hold me every night.

We had great sex; it was hard and rough and just the way I love it. In fact, the way he took me like he owned me proves he needed this. The sadness in his whisper when he first approached me went right through me.

He knows his way around a female body. His hands toyed with me, bringing me on the brink of intense pleasure all in a matter of a few seconds. It was brutal, intense, and exactly what we both needed.

Most women would feel used; hell, a typical woman would run as far away from a man who's still in love with another woman who will only ever be a memory to him, but I'm not your typical woman. I would never expect him to forget her or to stop loving her. And I'm not stupid enough to think this was anything more than a quick fuck.

What I am is a woman with needs of my own. I have my own burning desire to have a man drive me to the brink of insanity. I love sex. I want someone to take control of me and fuck me like he means it, yet not be afraid to let me take control every once in a while.

I'm adventurous, a tad bit on the kinky side. My past relationship was very sexual. I'm aware of what works for me and what I could live without. Beau seemed to know exactly what I liked.

Being a med student has its advantages, but many disadvantages drown those out. I know that the loneliness I've been dealing with disappeared the minute he slammed his mouth on mine. At first, I was shocked he could go from hating me to attacking me like that, but the taste of pure male invaded my senses and all I wanted him to do was take over and fuck me. If I can help him have a night away from his own torture, then it's a win for both of us. No-strings-attached affection that we both definitely needed.

I squirm, and my eyes fly open when he moves slightly. On instinct, I peer up at him. The guilt is there even though he tries to hide it with a tight, forced smile. I want him to be himself around me and feel comfortable enough to say whatever is on his mind. I'm not going to go bat shit crazy if he says he regrets what we did. It'll hurt a little, but I'll get over it. I can't deal with the guilt that's radiating off of him as he looks at me. I don't mind being a much-needed release when he needed it, but what I won't be is a regret he has to deal with on a daily basis.

This is when the rational side of my brain tries to kick in, trudging its way through the heavy fog until clarity is all that remains. Beau needs to come to terms with this himself. I can give him a slight shove in the right direction and maybe be the friend he said he didn't need and listen if he brings it up. I don't know. All I do know is, right now, he needs to be let off the hook in a big way, and I need to make sure he knows I'm good with everything that happened.

"Good morning." I yawn, then move away from him. I'll be the one to ease his mind. I can't stand the way he's looking at me like he's trying to figure out what to say.

"Listen, Beau, don't read anything more into this okay? We had sex. It doesn't have to complicate the fact you're an asshole. No need to regret anything that happened. I'm not expecting anything out of all of this." I have to tease him and try to deflect some of this tense awkwardness in the room. I'd give anything to hear him laugh like he did with the guys last night. He needs to smile more; it's very sexy on him.

He also needs to quit looking at me like he can't believe he heard me correctly. It's me who smiles when it takes him all of five seconds to let the air out he must have been holding and the deepest laugh escapes his lips. Lips I would love to have over mine again right now. Lips I want to bite and lick. But instead, I'll just watch them while the two of us go back to getting under each other's skin.

"You have no idea how fucked up I am. Hell, every day bleeds right into the next for me. As far as us having sex, I'm not a bullshitting type of guy, nor am I one to disrespect a woman. I have a lot of guilt over last night, Emmy, but to prove to you I'm not as big of an asshole as you think I am, I'm being honest when I say I don't regret it."

He shrugs. What he fails to understand is whether he's using me or not, who am I to complain about being fucked by a man who clearly knows how to please a woman?

I don't have time to think about anything more before he grabs me by the waist and hauls me up over his body. This guy is built. He's fucking gorgeous, and the want in his eyes excite me.

"Are you asking me if you can fuck me again?" I breathe out heavily as his erection rubs against my clit. My eyes are focused on his beautiful eyes. There's something there today, unlike all the other days where he seemed empty.

"No. I'm telling you I *am* going to fuck you again. Then we're both going to shower, get out of this house, and do something. I don't care what the hell we do as long as we get the fuck out of here. I need out of this house."

"Hmm. You think my brother will let me leave?" I exhale sharply as he thrusts upwards, grinding against me. I'm wet and aching from the way he's moving against me. I need more. I need to touch him and let him make me come undone, then I'll watch him follow.

"Your brother has been on my ass to get out of here. Let's take a walk. Jade told me there are trails around here."

"Okay, but first I need a shower," I tell him as I slide down his body. My eyes have to be showing him disappointment that we aren't going to continue what we've started. He lifts a brow as I stand in front of him naked.

"Give me just a few minutes and I'll be out." I can hear him following me before I even get through the bathroom door. He reaches around me and turns on the hot water as his other hand slides down my side.

"I guess I'm not finished with you. You made me hard as hell when you walked away from me." His deep voice over my shoulder sends chills over my otherwise naked body.

"I won't kick you out of the shower if you want to join." His laughter makes me smile, and I can feel his cock moving against my ass.

"Well, it's nice to know you won't throw me out. Fuck, your brother would kill me if he knew what I was about to do to you."

"I'm not about to tell him." I slide my hand around and grip his cock in my hand, squeezing until he exhales with me. His little moan sends us into another desperate race to get into each other's arms until my legs are wrapped around his waist and we're both moving against the wall. The water scalds my chest all the way down my stomach, but I don't dare say a word. Fuck, this is hot.

"You're so tight." He closes his eyes as he fucks me. I know he's not truly with me in this moment, and I understand that he just needs this from me. He makes me feel so good that I just grip his shoulders and let him slide me up and down the wall until we're both moaning through another orgasm. I watch him as he finishes and opens his eyes at the very end.

There it is. Guilt again. But I don't let him know I saw that. I simply move around him and grab the soap. I take it upon myself to lather him up and force him to let me do this for him. He doesn't really try to fight me, just needs a little encouragement as I move around him and get his back.

I let my fingers run over the ridges in his body and can't help but appreciate what I touch. He's sexy as hell, there's no doubt about that, but he's a broken soul, and sometimes that is something you can't overcome or compete with.

He leaves the shower once he finishes his hair, leaving me to do my own thing. I appreciate that, because I'm not really keen on shaving and doing the whole cleanup thing with someone watching my every move.

"What is that?" I ask a focused, clean-scented Beau when I enter the kitchen an hour later. We may be out in the middle of nowhere, but a woman still has to primp. I showered, shaved, applied a tinge of makeup, and dried half of my hair, making it easier to pull it back into a basic braid that's swung over my shoulder. I even found an old Army tank top of Kaleb's in one the dressers. It's a little big, but at least it won't be sticking to my skin when we walk in this sweltering heat. Top it off with a pair of black workout shorts and tennis shoes, and I'm ready to go on this walk.

"It's a Remington XM3." He places the rifle back into a case then swings it across his shoulders. I gulp. I may know how to shoot a gun and actually love doing it, but that damn thing looks dangerous.

"Should I be worried about going into the woods with you?" I tease him, hoping we can actually do this walk without any awkward weirdness about what happened last night and again this morning.

"No. What you should be worried about is what I'm going to do with you when you lose." He bends and grabs a big jug of water, a backpack, and my gun case.

"Lose what?" I ask as I follow him out the door, grabbing the jug from his hand when we step off the porch.

"Thanks." He flips the case into his other hand then moves a little closer to me as we both make our way across the lot to the back of the house. "I saw you shooting the other day, thought maybe we could do a little target practice. Who knows, maybe place a wager to see who hits their mark first." I stop walking, and he watches me with a huge smile on his face.

"That's a little unfair, don't you think? I mean, you're in the Army. You're Special Forces, for God's sake." *A sexy as hell badass.* I shoot only to keep my aim perfected. No way can I hit a target dead center like he can.

"Well, I'll tell you what, Emmy. I'll drop the bet and we'll do it for fun then. But if I win, I think you'll still just have to pay up. Maybe I can think of some sexual favor you can perform to pay up your debts."

"We can maybe work something out, but get ready if I beat you. You'll have a debt to pay yourself. I may have an idea up my sleeve." I nod in agreement as I respond to him and don't miss the hunger in his eyes as I keep talking. The sexy smile on his face and the way he's standing there has me truly questioning my sanity at the moment. I'm literally playing with fire when it comes to him. I can feel it.

For the first time in a very long time, I believe I've found a man I could fall for, and that scares the living shit out of me.

CHAPTER SEVEN

HARRIS

The minute she left me with a satisfied dick was the minute I sprang into action. I dressed in fifteen minutes and actually looked forward to spending the day with someone. I feel good, relaxed, and better than I have in a long time. I'm being honest with myself when I say I'm thinking with my dick when it comes to her. She looks like a goddamn fantasy created just for me in that loose tank top with ARMY written across the underside of her tits and those shorts that sculpt her tight ass.

My brain is reactivated for some screwed-up reason. It more than likely has everything to do with the words she easily let tumble out of her mouth when she told me it was basically no strings sex, then topped it off with me still being an asshole, which undoubtedly I am.

She eased my conscience and took my words right out of my mouth, surprising the hell out of me. If she's game for some straight-up fucking, then who the hell am I to complain? She needs to be quiet about this whole thing though; the last thing I need is for Kaleb to be all over my shit about his sister.

If I had a sister, I'd keep her as far away from a man like me as I possibly could. Hell, most men have been known to use women for their own personal needs. I mean, fuck, I don't know shit about her, and she could be using me as much as

I'm using her. Frankly, I couldn't give a shit if she is, but her brother, he's a masochist when it comes to protecting his family, and even though Kaleb has been trying to get me out of my head, I highly doubt he meant for me to bury my cock between his sister's legs. We may be friends, but the guy is overly protective of his family.

He has every right to protect those he loves. It's his right. I'm just not prepared to tell him any of it yet. I'd hate to lose him as a friend. The guy has been by my side for so much in such a short time.

My phone rings and what do you know, it's Jade.

"What?" I mumble.

"Fuck you too," she barks out like the little bossy shit she can be.

"What are you up to today?" How quickly her mood can change. That's Jade, one minute she will pull a gun on you, the next she's sounding all concerned.

"Eh. Emmy and I were talking. She told me she knew how to shoot, thought maybe I'd head out to the woods somewhere, do a little target practice." It's the truth. This way when they all hear guns going off, they won't think we're under attack and come out there and shoot us both.

"Are you sure you should be handling a gun right now?" she says in her concerned tone. What in the ever loving fuck? I may have been grieving, but I sure as hell have never given her or anyone the opinion I'm suicidal or postal. If that's what she means. She knows me better than that. Her insinuating

I'm anything but professional around guns pisses me off. I step out around the house and away from the porch so Emmy won't hear me set Jade straight. This isn't an easy task, and I'm sure it won't be pretty.

"You have a hell of a lot of room to talk about a person handling a gun. I remember all too well that you pointed one directly at my head in Mexico." I address her with the truth as well as hostility in my voice.

"That was entirely different, and you know it," she whispers the guilt through the phone.

"The circumstances were, yes. My point is, people do crazy shit when they lose something they love. I can promise you, Jade, this is something I need. I may feel dead inside, Jade, but I sure as hell am not going to do something stupid," I articulate in a way I hope she understands. I need space. I need to blow off steam. And pulling the trigger of a gun is what I need right now, whether she likes it or not. It's a part of me, and I need to find me again.

"I'm sorry. I care about you and worry about you."

"I know you do. Just trust me on this. Take it as a step in my healing. You've all been on my ass for weeks to get out and do something."

"I can do that. Just please don't shut me out anymore." Defeat is all I hear in her voice. It pisses me off that I had to ask her to give me space. This is Jade. She's the one person I usually tell everything to, and now I can't seem to look at her without thinking of what I've lost.

"I'll work on that. I promise."

We hang up with everything fine between us. But still, I wonder now how screwed up everyone thinks I am. I don't even know the answer to that myself.

~~~

"How much further?" Emmy suddenly turns around, which causes me to run right into her. Her chest smashes up against mine. "I have no idea. Never been out here before." I take a look around at our surroundings.

"Damn," I say. Her head shifts to the side, then she turns and catches her breath.

"Holy shit. This view is unbelievable," she gasps. My grip on her gun case hardens. I've been lost in thought thinking about how good it's going to feel to have my gun in my hands for I don't know how long, while this scenery has been all around me? It's magnificent. If I were a hunter, I'd be in heaven. We're deep into the woods. Cascades of light peak through the openings at the top of the trees. A large open field is a little way ahead. The smell of the damp green grass mixed in with the musty fragrance of mother earth with the dark and clay-colored dirt. The smell of pine and oak gives off the aroma that the rebirth of spring is almost here.

"It's beautiful out here. A little too dark to shoot a gun. Let's walk a little further." I lift the case I'm clinging to and point it toward the clearing.

"Are you alright? You've been quiet." Her head whips back in my direction, bringing with it that braid that fills my head with all kinds of debauched ideas on what I'd like to do to her.

I brought some water and a few snacks in case we needed them. I guess we were both a little too anxious to get out of there that neither one of us mentioned breakfast.

"I'm good, Emmy. Just thinking."

We finally reach the wide-open area where the outlining of trees on the other side will make perfect targets. I pause to take one lingering look at her nicely-shaped ass before I speak and ask her to stop. "This looks like a good spot for you to get your ass kicked all over these woods." I sit the case down in the open field. The sun isn't as intense as it has been, yet it feels nice. I drop the backpack as well as lift the strap of my rifle case over my shoulder, being careful when I place it down.

"Okay then. Let me show you how to shoot a gun, Captain." She moves proudly to the case and begins to inspect the guns.

"I'm assuming Kaleb taught you." It's more a statement than a question.

"Of course, he did. He taught mom too. She's a damn good shot. I guess you could say it runs in the family. I practice any chance I get, which hasn't been much lately with school." I listen intently. Fucking hell, I never realized how much I've missed having a normal conversation with someone until I started to listen to her talk about something I'm actually passionate about.

"You have no idea the things I can do." Her brows lift in a mocking way. Her innuendo shoots straight to my dick. Emmy hands me the jug of water, which I take and down some of it instantly. It feels good going down my throat after that hike. I've deprived my body of everyday nutrients for way too long. *That shit is another change I have to make.*

"Show me what ya got?" Ignoring her little remark, I hand her back the water and find myself watching her a little too closely as she takes a few gulps.

"You've already seen everything I've got." She wipes her mouth with the back of her hand, and I shake my head.

"Not talking about your body, Emmy. I'm talking about shooting that pistol I saw you holding the other day."

"Spying on me?"

"Nah. Checking out the goods." I point at her gun case.

"Whatever, Beau Harris. I'm about to beat you down. Then we'll see who gets to hold the power and the bragging rights." With that, Emmy Maverick proceeds to take her mean-looking pistol out of her case, puts a pair of protective glasses on, then loads that bad bitch of a handgun. She does it all with perfection and with her ass in my periphery. She spreads her legs and takes a stance before she places her finger smoothly across the trigger. All I hear is the ping of the bullets hitting a tree, but what surprises me the most is watching a woman other than those I've trained with since I was eighteen years old have this kind of precision. My damn dick is hard just watching her.

"Tell me about yourself, Emmy?" She turns and looks at me with a strange expression.

"What would you like to know?" I shrug at her question. Has this woman never had anyone want to know who she is, what makes her tick?

"What made you decide to become a doctor?" I position my rifle just to look through my scope, dialing in until I find her target. Shit. She nailed it. "Nice shooting." I pull the trigger and hit the furthest target on our course. That's just the difference between a pistol and a rifle.

"I'm not sure. I've always wanted to help people. It also runs in the family, I guess." She speaks of it all so nonchalantly. We both grow insanely quiet until I peg out another tree.

"It takes a lot of patience to do what you're doing. I honor you for that." I lost the spark to talk to anyone about anything the day I lost Mallory. This is a little awkward, but I keep talking because she's actually the first person to intrigue me since that day. I'm not sure why I feel the need to talk to Emmy about anything at all. I just do.

"I think a man sacrificing his life for his country is the most honorable thing a person can do." I grow tense; my muscles stiffen. Not from her words, but because I truly do miss what I loved to do for so many years. I miss the adrenaline from hunting down the enemy and taking a successful mission home. I need back in the game.

I flash back to last night when Kaleb asked me if I was ready to help find the person responsible. I was hesitant at first, because honestly, I'm not sure I can handle it and stay level-headed when it comes to the mission surrounding Mallory.

"You miss it, don't you? I can see it in your face." She nails it. "You need to get yourself together and get back out there."

"I plan to. Just need some time." She stops talking as I admit out loud that I'm not in a good place.

"Time is different for everyone. Some find that work helps with the chaos." She turns and sends another round into the trees. Hearing her words starts to make me think more about going to work. I lose myself in the targets and let the chaos of my life float through my mind as I find peace in this. It's the best therapy I could've asked for.

I can find her killers. I can ruin them. It won't bring the two of them back to me, but it's a justice I have to see met.

I have a new outlook on this day and decide to make the most of my time here with Emmy. She looks at me with a teasing smile, and I wink at her. That only starts the fun while we begin to play.

For the next hour or so, we continue to shoot, the thundering crackle of the guns echoing as we continuously battle in this dangerous game of cat and mouse we play. Back and forth we tease and taunt one another to the point where she's pressing her tits to my back, tempting to distract me. I'm stroking my dick through my shorts to try and divert her eyes away from her target. Like me, she remains fearless and focused.

She's been trained well, and even though I want to throw her ass down in the grass and show her who's boss around here, I hold it in. I let my training take over and block out my surroundings, and every fire of my gun, every pull of the trigger has my sad cluster of a messed-up head remembering the sound, the way it feels to kill the enemy the first chance you get. It electrifies me, my body hums, and awareness sets in.

We may be playing a game by shooting guns out in the open, one no one should play unless they know what the hell they're doing, but this is the best kind of healing I need right now. Proving I can handle the sound of a gunshot is major improvement for me. And I feel better knowing I haven't lost my steady finger or aim.

I may not be trained like Jade in the sniper field, but I sure as hell have been taught in the best organized unit around. I'm a soldier, a United States Army specialist, and whoever is out there waiting for us to make a move better pray like a man on his knees. Captain Beau Harris is back, and I'm going to seek revenge, vengeance, and the satisfaction of blowing their goddamn heads off and pissing down their fucking necks.

CHAPTER EIGHT

EMMY

I know I'm a goner the minute I watch him begin to shoot his rifle. He's focused, and his muscles move perfectly as he hits the target. I've always found a man who could handle a rifle very sexy. He tries not to bring attention to his hard-on, which I'm not sure he got from watching me or from shooting his own gun. All I know is, I can't help but feel the smile grow wide across my face as I watch this man completely in his element after I've seen how torn he truly has been.

A part of me knows this is a big step for him. I can feel how much he's relaxed since we got out here.

I don't think either one of us is concerned about the bet anymore. This has turned into something else. It's training and healing for him, and as insane as it sounds, I'm happy to see this side of him. This is the guy Jade told me about, the kind and laid back Harris who would do anything for his friends and loves life.

"Harris is one of the best soldiers I've met. He needs to get back into the game. It's in his blood," she told me one day while talking on the phone. My response to her was to tell her I knew exactly how she felt. In a way I did. I proceeded to tell her how Kaleb was when he returned the last time from his final tour in Afghanistan. He wasn't my brother; he was void of emotion.

You couldn't touch him, let alone talk to him. Even though our circumstances are entirely different and my brother is still living, at the time, it felt like he was gone. The man who returned was not the same man who'd left. So I got it. I understood better than anyone how it felt to see someone you love become lost in themselves. You feel helpless; you tiptoe around them not knowing what to say or do, afraid to talk and yet needing to, because the love you have for them is so strong you want to do everything in your power to bring the person back. You love them, miss them, and hate to see them walk around like a stranger in the body of someone you once knew.

"You give up yet?" His sultry eyes skim up and down my body. His deep voice has my skin alert and ready to see what he plans to do next.

"I never give up, although I'll admit defeat in this. You're an amazing shot." I twist my body in his direction and purposely bend forward to give him the perfect view of my breasts as I grab my rag to wipe off my gun.

"Since I won and you seem to want to tease me with those perfect tits of yours, I want you to take that tank top off." I didn't realize he was going to try to do something out here, but honestly, the thrill of just thinking about it has me excited.

I finish what I'm doing, stand up, and drink him in from head to toe with a gaze that tells him I surrender. He can have all the control he wants right now as long as he does what his eyes are promising he's about to do.

I slowly slip my hands down my stomach until they reach the hem of the top, then seductively hoist it up over my head before letting it drop to the grass. His eyes stay glued to my chest. I didn't think my nipples could get any harder than they were this morning, but they just did. They both ache to be touched.

"If you love that lace bra, you better take it off now, or I'm ripping it right the fuck off of your body." Jesus, the way he's demanding me makes me want to drop everything and just let him take me without a chase, but I do like to play.

"You want these?" I have to tease him. I turn around and unsnap my bra, giving him a view of my back before I cup both of my breasts and turn around to face him. He's looking at me with a hunger I can understand, because I feel the same way looking at him.

"Pinch your nipples." I close my eyes and do what he says, still hiding them from his view. I pinch, rub, and almost lose control imagining what he's about to do to me. The rustle of his shorts dropping springs my eyes open again. I gasp when I see him stroking his cock.

"I told you before I'm not gentle. I like to fuck hard, Emmy. I'm going to fuck you. You're going to slide those tight shorts off, lie down in the grass, and let me watch you get that pussy ready for me. Use your fingers and tease me." Oh my God. I almost want to say 'yes, sir' to him from the way his voice demands me to move with urgency. He has me on edge, ready to explode, and he hasn't even touched me.

I let go of my breasts, shimmy my shorts down my legs and over my shoes, and lie down in the soft, long green grass. The sun shines brightly, yet the trees block it out from directly hitting me in the face.

"Spread your legs, wet your fingers. Let me see you." He drops to his knees in front of me all the while still stroking himself, never taking his eyes off of mine. I do what I'm told, expecting him to move his eyes to my fingers, but he doesn't. He's watching my reaction to all of this, and I can't tell you how sexy that is.

I'm wet and ready, and the longer this goes on, the more eager I'm getting to have him over me. My fingers slide into my heat, coating my fingers. When he finally directs his gaze to my hands, his nostrils flare as he takes in the vision of my fingers sliding in and out of me.

I'm on the verge of a climax; he senses it, grabs ahold of my hand, and leans in far enough to coat his dick with my arousal. Good God, this has to be the single most erotic thing I have ever done. I love it.

Without another word, he straddles me. That beautiful dick slides easily between my legs. He grinds into me, and we both begin to move in the grass as he thrusts his hips into mine over and over, each time getting deeper.

"Jesus Christ," he mumbles without ever slowing his hips from moving furiously. The friction is raw, primal, and leaves me completely incapacitated. All I can do is watch him as he fucks me like this is his last fuck. Hard and fast with a fury of desperation that is breathtaking to watch. The muscles in his neck twitch, and his tight ass is all I grip as he continues.

I know the moment he's ready to come when he starts to bellow out a string of incoherent words that has me arching my back, giving him the access to the deepest part of me. He pulls out quickly before he explodes, his cum coating my breasts and stomach. He looks different. There's a determination in his eyes I've not seen before.

"I didn't go inside of you, because I want to taste you. I want to taste what I've done to you, Emmy." He shifts his weight off my body and lifts my ass in the air effortlessly as he takes another look at me. The awkwardness of this is silenced by the fact I was so close to a release that I'm teetering on the edge, and he knows it. He blows just slightly, and I begin to squirm in his hands.

My hands are sprawled out flat on the ground. With one strong stroke of his tongue, he licks from the top of my opening all the way to my ass, then back up again. I scream his name when he bites my clit, sucking it hard into his mouth.

"Oh my God. Beau!" I yell out as I moan. He's relentless. His stroking and sucking sends me clawing at the grass in an attempt to get a grasp on reality. Fighting against his hold as he presses his tongue onto my clit and nibbles it again, I almost lose it. I feel him lay me back down on the ground before his hands go to my thighs, pushing them outward. His fingers delve into my pussy while his tongue teases my clit, and he sends me swirling around a release so violent I'm not sure my body can take it.

I want more. I grip his hair and grind into his face. He's pressing his tongue into me with the same desperation, and I'm so fucking close. He keeps up the pace, and I don't stop grinding against his facial hair. The second he bends his finger inside of me is when I let go and come. Harris doesn't stop though; he keeps going, fucking me with his mouth and fingers until he draws one more long, hard orgasm out of me before he stands up.

He turns away from me and pulls up his pants with haste and frustration. It leaves a ping of guilt in my chest as I watch him move around the space, never once looking back at me. I know this is fucking with his head, and I hate that I can't stop it for him.

"You ready to head back?" His voice is deep, and his dick is showing hard through his shorts. He slides his shirt off and tosses it to me. "Use it to clean yourself up." He finally looks right at me when I sit up and take the shirt from his hands. There's no smile. No emotion. Nothing.

It's as if something has shifted in the clean air out here. Like a storm is brewing deep within his soul, and I know there's no reaching him. I know what he said this is, that he has nothing left inside of him to give. He has more to give than he thinks. I can see the pain in his eyes and know he's still feeling. He's not dead inside. It's what he lost he can't get past. Who can blame him?

What he said about never forgetting them earlier sits right there on my heart. I want to console him and make him feel better, but I know there's nothing I can say to make that hurt lessen, and I can only imagine that I'm the source of some guilt he's trying to work through.

He's struggling with all those inner demons he has. The guilt, shame, and betrayal he feels. I can't help him with any of that, but what I can do is keep his mind occupied on something else. Something that has nothing to do with sex.

He helps me stand by holding out a hand for me to take. I make quick work of getting dressed and gathering my things while I remain quiet. It's odd in a way after what we just did for neither of us to speak or for him to shift gears and go from dominating my body to shutting himself down as if nothing happened and that I disgust him.

I have to give him his space. The sincere thing is, I like this guy and want to get to know him. I'd love to discover the things he likes and dislikes outside of the bedroom. I think it's clear we have a lot in common when it comes to sex, but other than that, I really don't know much about him.

"I'll wash my shirt," he tells me as he takes it from where I sat it on my case and shoves it in his bag. He hoists his bag over his shoulder and doesn't speak as he begins to walk again. I follow him quietly, trying to decide if I should break the silence. I'm one to speak my mind when I feel the time is right, therefore, I go for it.

"So. Beau. Tell me about you? I know you're in the ARMY. You've known Jade for a while. Do you have any siblings? Are your parents still around?" I know he has a mother. I remember seeing her sitting beside him at the funeral. I really don't recall seeing anyone else, not that I was looking. I tried to focus on Jade and my brother. Even though my heart was breaking for the man sitting in the front pew with his shoulders slumped and his head lowered.

"It's just me and mom. She adopted me when I was two. Her husband left her for another woman before I came around. She's retired from teaching fourth grade in Tallahassee, where I grew up. She lives in Zepherhills now, which is a small retirement community." His answer is short and doesn't give away any more than the simple answer to my question.

"The two of you must be close. I bet she's very proud of you and all you've accomplished." I step over a large tree branch and halt when he stops a few feet in front of me.

"Look. I get what you're trying to do here, making small talk, trying to get me to think about something else. It won't work. This up here," he taps his head, "is not interested in talking about my mom. Yes, she's proud, and yes, she's worried about me. I don't want to make small talk. I've fucked up, and now I need to deal with some bullshit before I fuck up even more. So please leave me alone before I say something I don't mean."

I don't know what it is that has my heart constricting in my chest. The way he's looking at me with those eyes that are stirring crazy thoughts, dreams, or whatever he has running through his mind is enough for me to say the hell with this. I'll be cordial, play the good girl for the sake of his sanity. What I won't do is allow him to fuck me like he can't live another second without me, then treat me worse than the dirt we're walking on. The pissed-off part of me wants to slap him, while the logical part of me keeps my mouth shut and follows him without another word.

"I'll be damned. How the hell did you get him out shooting?" Steele strolls out of the office with his handsome looks and confident approach. He's changed so much in all the years I've known him. Going from a buzz cut to long hair, from a smooth face to a beard. One thing that hasn't changed is the way his eyes can pierce through your soul. Or the way he flirts with those eyes that could suck you in.

"She didn't. It was my idea. Felt fucking great to shoot. I needed it." Beau's tone is on the verge of shitty.

"How's the shoulder?"

"A little tight, but much better. Is everyone in there?" Beau lifts his chin toward the office. I'm not sure if Steele notices Beau's change in demeanor, but I do. His eyes start shifting back and forth. He's debating whether to go in there or not. I have no idea if they've found what they're looking for. I know it has to do with the murder. None of these men will give up until they find out who it is and why. They will seek justice. Basically, they will kill whoever took one of their own. There's no other way around it.

Kaleb has enemies. Each one of these men do. Hell, Jade probably does as well. It could be a million people who have decided now is the time to seek out revenge, which makes you strike out in the worst way. They wanted to hit them where they least expected it but where it hurt them the most. If this is about revenge, then it must be against Beau, or against the entire team combined.

"Some valuable information came in early this morning. I was heading over to see if you were up to seeing it instead of waiting until Monday. We all agreed you should know." I swallow. I hope and pray he takes another step. It may seem harsh and fast as a lot has happened to create fear and havoc on Beau's emotional state in the past twenty-four hours. I believe in him. He can do this. Both of us stand there for a few minutes, watching Beau battle back and forth with the side of him that's searching deep to see how much strength he has left.

Everything is tightly hidden inside of him. His shield is back up, putting more pressure on him to either snap at this information he is being told or to bear the pressure and go find the killer. Both Steele and I watch him, watching the battle turning into a war he's caught in the middle of.

I feel a little weak in the knees from witnessing a tormented man deciding if he has the strength or not. It hurts me to see him this way. It's when he walks past me, up the few stairs that lead into the office when Steele gives me a look that tells me he feels it too.

CHAPTER NINE

HARRIS

Whoever the hell said there's light at the end of a tunnel is full of it. As hyped up as I was earlier about feeling good, seeing the light and all that crap is gone. I'm lost in the back of my mind again. A few words out of Emmy's mouth were all it took to trigger my thoughts right back to Mallory.

I know I fucked up with her when I ripped her head off. I just can't stop the chaos that snapped straight into my mind when I closed my eyes and imagined Mallory. When I opened my eyes, I realized I was only dreaming and felt like shit for being with another woman when all I was thinking about was Mallory.

I hate that I snapped at her. All because she wanted to get to know a little something about me. Wasn't she doing the same thing I was earlier when I asked her questions about herself? I'm worse than an asshole. I'm a fucking idiot to talk to her like that or to any woman for that matter, and now I'm standing here in the throes of possibly finding out who in the hell was behind all of this and can't concentrate for shit. I'm ready to explode. I have the itch to kill a motherfucker or something, not that it would make any of this any better.

"Hey." Jade moves up beside me, her hand reaching for my arm. I tug away from her before she has the chance to make contact. I can't afford to be distracted any more than I already am. I need to be focused.

"I'm good," I lie, like I've been doing for months now, knowing damn well she isn't buying anything I say and neither is anyone else. Fuck them all. I need to know what they've found out. I'm not here for a therapy session.

"You're not good, brother. You look like shit. You're sweating, and your body is shaking. Maybe you're not ready for all of this. Why don't you let us have solid proof before we show you anything?" I toss my stuff on top of one of the desks and run my agitated, shaking hands through my hair, while Kaleb and I stare each other down after he more than likely asked Steele to come looking for me. Now, when he sees how screwed up I am, he thinks he can change his mind. I don't fucking think so. I'm fucking here. This is what he's been trying to make happen for days. It's time to get to the bottom of this, so I can find the motherfucker who ruined my life.

"What the hell are you trying to hide from me, man?" I see nothing but guilt. His face is peppered in it.

"Kaleb, no," Jade interjects a little too quickly for me, but before I get a chance to respond, Kaleb jumps in.

"Show him, Steele," he says, and I hear Jade gasp beside me, papers shuffling, and then the sound of heavy footsteps getting closer to me. Those steps hold my life. What I'm about to see is either going to break me, or it's going to lead me in the direction I need to heal. With shaky hands, I grab the papers, close my eyes, and take a deep breath. Not a damn thing I do prepares me for what I see in front of me.

"You have got to be fucking kidding me?" I bellow out. The letterhead from USSOCOM, where Steele used to work before he decided to help on our missions by piloting the planes and choppers, has one sentence stating there are still no suspects. I flip to the next one from the FBI. Same thing. This can't be right and yet it is. It's staring me in the face.

Those vague sentences have me wadding up the papers and hurling them as far as I can throw them. "Fuck all of this shit. I need some answers. Tell me you're joking."

"I wish I were, man. We can't find a thing. No clues, no reasons. Nothing. We've been on this since it happened. Steele has a buddy of his working day and night on this, Harris, and that doesn't count the endless hours we're all putting into it." This is why he looks guilty, why they all do. They've all been busting their asses to try and find the murderer of the woman I loved, while I've been wallowing in my self-pity and barely hanging on. My friends have been in here pulling strings and busting their balls to only come to a dead end every fucking time.

"We're missing something. Something that's more than likely right in front of our face," Steele speaks up. I close my eyes and take deep breaths, exhaling slowly, trying to clear my head. I'm trying so hard to wrap it around the fact I may never know why my life was ripped from my arms. I force calmness and try to make myself see what could be that one missing piece I know they don't.

I open them slowly when I feel Jade's small but firm hand on my arm. The guilt and pain radiating off of her buckles my knees. I look from her to everyone in this room, their faces resembling each other's. This is bullshit. None of them should feel guilty. Hell, if I'm being reasonable here with trying to pull my life back together, I shouldn't feel that way either. This is none of our faults. The only one or ones to blame are the fuckers who did this. The hollow feeling in this room ends here.

"I want to see everything. Every person, every angle you have looked at. Whoever started this doesn't have the power over us. I see the look on all of your faces. It's the look I've been carrying around for months. Guilt doesn't belong in this room. What does, is our experience to figure this out. The missing key is out there, and we're going to find it." I swallow the lump in my throat and try to stare into the eyes of each one of these friends who have given up their lives to do a job I should have been a part of all along.

They've given me time to grieve. I'll mourn for the rest of my life, but I will never be at peace and neither will they until we, as a team, bring whoever is behind this straight to the gates of hell.

"Take a seat. It's going to be a long day, brother." Kaleb never takes his eyes off of me as he begins opening file after file. He's scoping me out like any good friend would. He needs to make sure I'm ready to handle this.

"I wouldn't be here if I weren't fucking ready. Now, quit looking at me like that and show me the shit I've missed." I'm straight up telling him the truth.

"I see that," he says with only the arrogance that can come from a man like him. *Cocky fucker.*

"I'm going to go make some coffee. I'll be right back," Jade says shakily. I know that tone. She's worried about me.

"I'll take water instead," I tell her. The corner of her lip quirks up. She's been at me to drink water for about as long as she's been on my ass to eat and shower. I notice the minute her face falters into a peaceful aspect of the Jade I used to joke around with. The only difference in her expression now is the sadness in her eyes. One I hope I can finally take away and replace with the icy, hardass glare that fits her call name of Ice she deservingly has.

"I'll help," Kaleb says to her, giving me my clear sign to walk away. I move around the two of them, heading for the table in the middle of the room with a couple of laptops open, where Jackson and Steele are pulling up different files.

"Everything from the government is in here. Jackson has all of our information on his." I pull a chair out, turning it backward and taking a seat. Propping my elbows on the back of the chair, I begin to read the first of hundreds of pages.

I scan through names, dates, and photographs of possible suspects. They have everyone in here, dating all the way back to my first girlfriend to a rival named Audra Shilling, who Mallory didn't seem particular fond of in high school. There isn't a beat missed here. I have no idea how long I sit there uninterrupted as I look from one computer to the other. Everything seems to match up.

What the government sent, these guys followed up on and vice versa. There isn't anything out of place. All the potential suspects have cleared alibis. The crime scene was scanned. Not that they found anything at a scene of a crime where a sniper shot into a place a million other people had walked the same route as her and I did that day.

The investigative puzzle leads to a building across the street from where we were exiting the doctor's office, where the sniper sat while he waited for us to come out of our monthly appointment. I fist my hands at the sight of the small apartment the piece of shit broke into. The room seems to fall quiet all around me as I scan the place out, seeking, searching, and scanning that open window as flashbacks flood my brain. It isn't until I notice the Medical Examiners Report that I stand up, shoving the chair out of my way, and enlarge the photo of the bullet that killed her that has me seeing red. My head snaps clear of every damn thing that has been plaguing it for months.

"Did you find something?" All the guys are right by my side. It's Kaleb who speaks and also places his hand on my shoulder, giving me a gentle squeeze.

"That's the same bullet I was shot with. Look at the orange tip. Those bullets are rare. Extremely rare. There's no fucking way that's a coincidence. Please tell me you guys checked out the possibility this could be tied to what happened down in Mexico." Kaleb grits his teeth and winces. The muscles in his jaw are ticking with pure stress. I hate bringing the hell he went through up, but fuck, I have to be sure.

"We did check it out. The bullet, the type of gun used, all of it, man. If this was done by anyone working with his brother, then they know exactly what they are doing and who they are up against, Harris. Whoever did this has covered their tracks," Steele pipes in. I glance back at the bullet. I know these guys have done everything they can think of. The proof is in front of me. It's all over the place.

I can't stop looking at the bullet. I'm unsettled about that damn thing for some ungodly reason. Yes, a lot of people use their own hand-made ammunition; most of it sucks, because the majority of the people in this world shoot a gun for the right reason, for pleasure or hunting. Those that kill though, they have their own special ammunition, and if they want to leave a sign or a warning, then this is exactly how they do it.

No. It isn't a coincidence that this particular bullet that killed Mallory happened to be the same one that blew out my shoulder. I don't buy it for one second that it is.

What I don't understand is why the government would stay involved if they didn't believe this was some kind of conspiracy theory against this team of ours, or why they haven't investigated this more. Maybe they have, and it's something they can't talk about. Hell, it could be a mixture of anything. If the government is involved, then they have suspicions of their own; otherwise, this would have remained a case with the local authorities.

We may be an elite team of soldiers, but when it comes down to it, we don't have the kind of power they do. This team knows it too; that's why they've been busting day and night in here working alongside them. I could be wrong about all of this, but something eats away at me.

"We need to get approval to take a trip to Mexico." I swipe my hands roughly through my hair until they land on the back of my neck where I clasp them together.

"Man, you better tell us what the hell you're thinking right now. There's no damn way the Army is going to let you leave the country. Not until you're permanently cleared. We sure as hell can't just fly across the border either. They've shut our go-to place down. It's been destroyed. All that's left are a few shacks." Steele pauses in his rant as I stand up.

"I've been medically discharged. I don't have to answer to them anymore. Fuck, I don't know. I have nothing to go on except a damn gut feeling, but I swear to Christ this has Mexico written all over it. Make it happen, Kaleb, get us down there." I walk away from the table with frustration that I haven't done any of this sooner.

"Your superior has discharged you knowing you're working with me. He left it so that if you decided to come back and were cleared psychologically, then he'd work the system to get you back in. Until then, you answer to me."

"Great, so let's fucking go now."

"What makes you think I'd clear you for something like this?" He stands to meet me face-to-face with nothing but seriousness across his face.

"You will clear me, because even in the most fucked-up state you were in, I had your damn back to go in and do what needed to fucking be done. Were you mentally there? Fuck, no. But sometimes you need this anger and fucking rage to get the job done. You'll either come with me as a team, or you can guarantee I'll go solo." Our glares become like an entire conversation as we stare at each other and read the expression on the other's face. I'm positive he knows I'm dead serious as well.

"Your ass won't go solo. I get it. I understand your desire to go do this yourself, but I think I need to send in some of the other guys first."

"Fuck off. I need this. I've sat cooped up for far too long. It's time I do something, even if it leads to a dead end."

"We don't even know for sure there's anything there."

"We know there are piece of shit assholes there. I'd like to rid the world of a few more if given the damn chance."

"Well, by all means, fucking send him in to shoot up Mexico. That won't go unnoticed," Steele talks over Kaleb, and we both turn to face him.

"What the fuck is your problem, Steele?" I move closer to him as my words spew anger at him.

"This isn't how we run shit. We go in and get out quietly and never leave a trace behind. You're not in the right mind to go in on something like this yet. I'll go and consider this saving your fucking life."

"Don't even think about keeping me from going, Fire. This is my fight." My rage radiates from me as I challenge him in my stare.

"Give the guys twenty-four hours to pull more information. We'll decide who's going in, but Harris…" He pauses until he moves even closer to me. "You will follow orders on this, or I'll restrain your ass to make sure of it."

"Don't try to leave me here and you won't have an issue." He's stubborn, but so am I. I'll accept his challenge any damn day of the year. The Army may have left me in his care, but not one of them will do a thing to stop me from seeing this through. Every one of these guys has been trained to follow through on a hunch, especially if it's personal.

CHAPTER TEN

EMMY

I enter the house after watching Beau's retreating back until he disappeared behind the door to the main office. I stand still for the longest time with my body plastered to the back of the door. The man is a tyrant in his own way. Something set him off, and I have no clue what. I shouldn't give a shit either, but I do, and that right there pisses me off more than anything.

I've never let a man get under my skin like this before, especially in such a short period of time. It has nothing to do with wanting to save him from himself or to help him get back to who he used to be. It has everything to do with wanting him. I find myself wanting to know all there is to know about him.

"Well, one thing you know is, he has a tongue that works magic and a dick he knows how to use." I start talking to myself before I move toward the kitchen.

Oh, I know all too well he's using me for nothing but a fuck, and I welcome it. Today in the field, I practically begged him to do it with the way I teased and taunted him the entire time. And now look where I am. I'm left feeling sorry for myself for the first time because of the way he fucked me then ducked me. Quite frankly, I hate this unwelcome feeling after a man fucks me. What did I expect to happen? It's just downright stupid, and yet I would go back for more, faster than a blink of an eye.

I groan because here I am, wanting to know everything about a man who is haunted by a past I don't even know how to tiptoe around. I can't comprehend the pain he's endured and will throughout his life as he continues to live without them.

"You need to stop, Emmy. Give the man the space he needs." I'm smart enough to know when I've pushed a little too hard and stepped over boundaries that are not mine to explore.

I leave the kitchen and head down the hallway to my room and shoving the thoughts of the day to the back of my mind. I kick off my shoes once I'm inside the large walk-in closet then place my gun case on the top shelf. My mood is shit, so I pull a yellow jersey wrap sundress off the hanger and make my way into the bathroom to shower before going to see my mom.

After turning on the shower, stripping my clothes off, and stepping in to let the water beat down my back, I begin to slowly relax. My mom is quick witted and smart as a whip. She will pick up on my frustrations if I don't wash them away. So that's what I try to do. I shampoo and condition my hair, wash away the scent of sex and everything Beau, and try to finish quickly.

I pick up my dirty clothes after deciding to let my still wet hair hang loose down my back, knowing if I put it up, it will take forever to dry. In less than a half hour, I'm walking across the compound in a pair of flip-flops, a bottle of chilled wine in my hand, and a smile on my face.

"Mom," I call out as I enter the house.

"Back here," she hollers. I follow the trail of her voice to the back of the house, where I find her sitting in the screened-in porch. Her legs are propped over the side of the chair, and her digital e-reader is in her hand.

"What are you reading?" I ask then sit down on the cool leather sofa across from her.

"A book that has some very hot sex in it." My mouth drops.

"Mother," I say a little stunned.

"What? I may not be getting any, but that doesn't mean I can't read about someone else getting a big, hard…"

"Stop. God. I came over to visit. Maybe I should examine your head while I'm here." This gets the two of us laughing so hard I end up buckling over and holding my now sore stomach.

"Hmm," she says and taps her finger on her chin. "You got some sun today. Out shooting with that sexy friend of Jade's, I heard. How is he, by the way?" My stomach flips from her speaking about Beau. And damn that Jade for opening her mouth to the one woman who knows me better than anyone. Although, when I study her, she doesn't have suspicion in her gaze; it's the look of sympathy that's written all over her face.

"I'd say he's in between the depressed and acceptance stages." I shrug. I'm familiar with all the stages of grief both from school and the loss of my brother, Ty. I've been through them all over the years. Right now, Beau is depressed and angry. Both are tough stages in the mourning process.

"There's no normal way to grieve, sweetie. We all do it differently. I'm still not over the loss of your brother. I never will be." Tears form in her eyes. I came over here to chat with her about anything but this. I've watched her cry over him enough. I'm not doing it anymore.

"Mom," I say quietly.

"I'm okay, really, I am." She swipes the tears from her face. "This isn't about me. It's about him and his loss. Jade is worried sick over him. I hate seeing her so upset. I wish I could help him, you know? I did see him walk into the office a while ago. From what Kaleb has said about him, I'm assuming it's the first time he's taken a step in there since everything happened. That speaks volumes, Emmy." She's right. It does. Beau has desensitized himself. He's shut every emotion off. I've figured this out in the short time I've known the man. Him walking in there today to find out whatever it is they strongly wanted him to know shows he is healing, whether he senses it or not.

"Yes, he did. I'm assuming you know why we're here then." I state more than question. She more than likely knows more than I do, which is next to nothing.

"Sure do. I would much rather be home, but it's nice spending time with the two of them even if their minds are elsewhere." I sigh and lean back, my still damp hair coating a cool moisture across my skin.

"Mom." We both jump at the sound of Kaleb's overbearing voice and the sound of his heavy boots thumping down the hallway in our direction.

"What's going on?" Her worry comes out from the sharp way she answers him. We stand when he stays in the doorway, imploring the two of us with hard, narrowed eyes to either sit back down or grab a hold of something to support us while we stand. Kaleb is angry, worried, and his defensive urge to protect us is rolling off of him tremendously. This is the first time I've really taken a long look at my brother. He's worn so much that the the slight wrinkles of everyday life appear more prominent at the corners of his eyes.

"You are scaring me, son. Did you find something? Is Stone, Harris, or whatever name you all call him alright?" It's not funny, therefore I inwardly laugh at how she calls him every name except his first name. I get it though. These call names they have for one another can baffle anyone's mind to keep them all straight. I stand watching them as she positions herself directly in front of him, giving him no choice but to look down at her. The minute he does, those heavy-lidded eyes so full of stress soften.

My brother is a decent man. He's our protector and is always looking out for the two of us. I have no idea how to go about doing the things he does. The one thing I know for sure is, he needs my help right now as he struggles internally to try and spit out whatever the hell is troubling him.

"Beau isn't handling whatever information you gave him, is he?" He looks from Mom to me. The second our eyes connect, it's as if he knows I'm trying to let him lean on me for once, to give him the out he needs to give Mom the basics of whatever has him distraught. I'm also conveying, 'It's me, your sister, and something is weighing heavily on your mind; say something to get her out of here so we can talk.'

"He's handling it better than I thought he would. I came in here to let you know that a few of us will be leaving to follow up on a lead in a few days. That's all the information I can give you at this point. I also wanted to ask if you wouldn't mind making all of us something to eat. I'm afraid it's going to be a long night for all of us." I sense he's telling the truth by the way he looks directly in her eyes when he speaks, but my brother is disturbed about something, and I have an inclination it has something to do with either where or why they are going.

"Of course, I will. I'll do whatever I can to help." Her comforting nature is a quality our mom has always had. She can ease into her role of taking care of the needs of others before her own without question. She also knows not to ask or pry Kaleb with questions when it comes to his job. I do too, except this time, I'm not about to keep my mouth shut. Not when whatever the hell is going on has him worked up on the inside to the point he's barely holding himself together.

"Thanks, Mom. Don't fuss too much over it. Something simple. I mean it."

"Simple, my ass, Son. If all of you are going to be at it all night, then you need some real food. Give me an hour or so." She leans in and hugs him tightly, places a kiss on his cheek, and saunters out of the room.

"You going to tell me what's really going on?" Kaleb lets out a low groan that I swear erupts from his heart and sears directly into mine.

"We've been busting our asses for months trying to find out who the hell did this, coming up empty handed every goddamn time, Emmy. He comes in there and looks over everything, and just like that, his gut tells him this all leads back to Mexico. I swear to God if this is tied to Ty in anyway at all, I will—"

"Stop, Kaleb, right the hell now. Don't you dare put the blame on your shoulders for the shit he did. You know better than anyone that a person who doesn't want help won't take it. I will not let you do this to yourself." Every muscle tenses in his upper body as he grips the doorframe. His eyes dart back and forth as my brother battles whatever demons are swarming their way inside of his body, trying to possess him in ways I cannot understand.

I'm sure the thought of any of his friends having to go to Mexico is killing him. That's the last place on earth Kaleb wants to think about. A part of me is praying it'll be someone else going and not him or Jade. It may sound selfish of me to think that, but this man standing in front of me is the only man who has ever loved me. Up until now, he has been my protector, my shield. It's about time the tables turn, because whether he wants it or not, I'm going to find out what's going on here and do everything I can to help.

"Let me help," I relay adamantly.

"You can help by not leaving Mom's side." His reply is exactly what I expect him to say. I would love nothing more than to be able to spend time with our mom. Not this time. Besides, she's fine with her sex books and all. Plus, she can use the down time to relax out here. He's gone too much to know she's constantly on the go. This is good for her, even though we are all trapped inside of this well-protected compound.

"Damn it, Kaleb, no. That's not what I mean, and you know it." Confusion crosses over his features as he takes in what I'm saying.

"Emmy, this is dangerous. There's no way in hell I'm letting you help with a damn thing." I'm not tucking my head between my legs this time like I always did when we were growing up and he would tell me he carried the burden of taking care of Mom and me. He always made sure I knew it was his responsibility and not mine.

"I'm not helpless, you know." His brows lift slightly, while his lips fight the spasm that seems to make him want to smile.

"I know that. I also know you went out shooting with Harris today. Not sure what the two of you talked about, but I do think whatever you did helped him. You using your psychological skills on him or what?" My heart starts to thumps rapidly. My brain begins to shuffle back and forth with the unknown truth behind the words he's saying to me.

I think before I speak, knowing my brother well. If I say the wrong thing or send vibes of what happened between Beau and me, my brother will freak the fuck out. The last thing he needs to know right now is his sister has been having the best sex of her life with a man who is using her.

"Something like that. You do have me staying with the man. It's kind of hard for us to not talk." I'm cautious of what I say to him.

"Well, you can help there then. Keep him talking, get him to open up. I'm afraid he'll draw back into himself until those guys get back here. If you can do that for me, then it would keep both mine and Jade's mind off of our biggest worry." Good God, if he only knew that talking is not the way I'll be helping.

"You know I'll do what I can." *It's just not in the way you're thinking.*

CHAPTER ELEVEN

HARRIS

Normally, a soldier is given somewhere in the vicinity of thirty days each year of leave time, unless hell breaks loose on their life like it has on mine.

I would be lying if I didn't admit that I miss everything there is about the Army, right down to the vigorous sixteen hours a day of pushing my body to the point of physical exhaustion. Mix that with how mentally drained I used to get, and I was often left physically and emotionally numb, but that was something I grew accustomed to after years and years of that. Now I know I'm capable of accomplishing any task I'm given inside or out of the military.

It's been months since I've used any form of my training, except for earlier today when I held my gun in my hand, which I owe to Emmy. She had no idea that watching her with that gun in her hand the other day had me craving to pick up mine just to prove to myself I could do it and that I could remember how to shoot.

I'd also be lying if I didn't admit to myself that I've thought about her the few times I've let my brain stray away from studying every bit of information that's been placed in front of me.

I owe her an apology. I was a fucking asshole to her. No one should be treated like shit when all they're trying to do is strike up a civil conversation with you, and I basically told her to lay off my ass and quit trying to get to know me; and that's after I fucked her and then walked away, leaving her behind like she wasn't worthy of any more of my time.

There's not a damn thing wrong with admitting that I like being around her and that when I get out of my own head, she's easy to talk to. We're actually compatible in a way that turns me on. She's sexy, both mentally and physically.

Am I a dick for what I did today? Hell, yes, I am, and the first chance I get, I'm apologizing to her and hope like hell she accepts it.

Hell, I don't know what to think right now. That's the problem; I've thought too much today. Seen too much in those files. Felt too much. And now I'm trying to process it all. How could all of this happen?

I'm left hanging in the office, watching all of my friends move around, multi-tasking and getting shit done. Things I need to be helping with, yet shit I don't give a fuck about, though I know I need to get back to it.

My scattered thoughts go back to Mexico and the bad vibes I've had that it all leads back there. It's nothing anyone has missed in what I know has been a thorough investigation. I had to explain it to Kaleb after he returned from storming out of here a few hours ago, claiming he needed to check on his mom and sister when we all saw the guilt and pain all over his face, thinking this could all be his fault.

The guy went through hell and back repeatedly in Mexico; hell, he ended up killing his own brother over it. And now it's eating him alive to think that his brother may have a helping hand still on earth to continue to drag him down. The fact that it's someone trying to get to him by killing an innocent woman.

Even though Kaleb and I had words, I saw the guilt in his eyes and felt the blame in his tone. Kaleb isn't to blame. None of us are. Once everyone set out to do the things they needed to, I pulled him aside to let him know I see it

It's the same damn thing I see and feel daily. It took me a half hour or so to get it through his stubborn head. Once I finished convincing him of that, the rough and demanding guy smiled, which made me think he was losing his mind until he spoke the words I didn't think I needed to hear until he said them.

"It's good to have you back, motherfucker, you level-headed son of a bitch." The room fell silent from his loud wisecrack before it filled with laughter as we all thought the same thing. Instead of him lecturing me on pulling my head out of my ass, it was me reversing the roles by explaining to him I would beat his ass if I saw one sliver of guilt from him for the life his fucked-up brother led.

It's my gut instinct that's telling me something in Mexico will put us on the right track to find the assholes who ruined my life and stole Mallory's. I just need to go and see it all for myself. Kaleb has to know how important this is to me.

"I want to see every single thing again. All the surveillance, all the reports, and even the shit you think isn't even important." I look to Pierce to pull the evidence back up. It's as though I finally leave my own body and look at it all from an outsider's mindset. Even though this is one of the hardest things I've ever done, it's what I need. Emotions tend to cloud a soldier's vision, which is why we are hardened.

"We just did that a minute ago."

"I'm not talking about the evidence on Mallory. I want Mexico. Everything we had from when Kaleb was there. I'm not leaving here until I've studied every fucking detail." Pierce gives me a look of acceptance and yells at Jackson to get the lights.

"I fuckin' love this stuff." Jackson settles in for the details, kicking his feet up on the table. He leans back in his chair, and we both watch as Pierce begins to show us everything from the last few missions.

It doesn't take long before Kaleb and Steele enter and we all get lost in analyzing it all.

"Who do we know of that was connected to Ty?" I have to ask and don't miss the feel of Kaleb's intensity shift as I do. This has to be as hard on him as it is on me.

"He had a few. One was Fernando Sanchez, who still hasn't been found; plus, we have a few females he was known to move around with. Al-Quaren, of course. And the further we dug, the more we realized he was in bed with fucking arms dealers all over the world." It could be any of them or someone entirely different. I'm not saying shit to get any of our hopes up until I have solid proof.

I keep my thoughts at bay and watch Pierce as he begins to pull out even more files as Jackson sets a beer next to each of us. I wasn't here for all of this information the first time, so it's good for me to see it all. Jade comes in when we have Kaleb's footage up, and I can feel her dying inside all over again. Her body begins to shake, and I can see her pain clear on her face. I hate to put her through this, but there is no way we can leave any angle out. I'm thankful when Kaleb grabs her hand while we watch it all play out again.

"I can't do this. Is it really necessary? I don't want to live through this shit again. Once was enough," she chokes out, then stands and walks behind the screen to busy herself as her feed begins to play out.

Shit, I remember that night like it was yesterday. I wanted more than anything to get to him before it was too late just to keep Jade from being destroyed. It's too bad we didn't have the same chance with Mallory.

"We're combing through all of this tonight. Harris wants to know all of this, and I can't see why we don't make sure he sees everything. Another set of eyes is just more of an asset for us when the team goes back," Jackson tries to explain logically to Jade, even though she already knows all of this.

This year has been hell on her. I fucking hate that I haven't been able to be there for her, but shit, I haven't even been functioning myself.

"I'll let you all do that then. Me though, I've seen them enough. I'm going to chill with the girls and see if I can help with dinner or something." I hear her, but my eyes never leave the screen as the guys all excuse her from staying.

What if it was these fuckers again? Some leftover piece of shit connected to Ty, a chick out for revenge, or a goddamn drug lord like Fernando? The thought of going back into that hell is the single worst thing I can think of in my life. The risk of losing another one of us will be more than any of us could take. It's obvious that whoever is behind this has private information on us. I mean, fuck, how would someone know where Mallory and I were that day if they didn't?

I'm not sure how long we sit there with our empty plates from dinner in our laps that Jade brought in. We ate and then watched for hours after looking at evidence, and my frustration grows. I feel lost and can't begin to fight the hopelessness that's stirring inside me. I stand as the last of the information flashes across the screen.

"Last one. This is the footage of the old man's house we stayed in. Just basic shit." Pierce puts the video on, and we all watch intently. My grip on my hair tightens as I take in the fact we have zero solid leads to go on, except my damn gut feeling.

"Fucking hell. I want to find the women Ty knew. If we have information on them, we can break them. Show them we know about their children if they have them, families, friends, or anyone they care about, and if they know anything, they'll fucking talk. They won't have the fucked-up mentality to take it to their grave like the damn scum we've been dealing with."

All the guys watch me as I begin to pace around the tables. "I'm not trying to say we actually hurt any of them, but they won't know that we won't." I stop talking when Jackson speaks up.

"Hell, sic Jade on them, and I'm positive they'll be scared for their damn lives." He starts to laugh before the rest of us do. I can see them all start to think about what I'm saying.

"What do we know about them?" I look to Pierce in hopes of some answers.

"I know one of them runs a resort with her father off the coast." As soon as his words come out, I know what has to be done.

"That's it. I'll go like I'm on a vacation. I can take Jade and go undercover." Kaleb scowls at me like I just stabbed him in his dick.

"Jade is not fucking going with you to Mexico. If she goes anywhere, I'll be right with her ass." Christ, the man is so damn possessive of her I'm surprised he doesn't shackle her ass to him when they sleep. I could stand here and argue with him about this, but instead, I'll just roll with it.

"Perfect. I'll take someone too and make it look like we're vacationing. Then we see what happens. Maybe we can pull some information out of these girls if they have any." My brows lift right along with his. Then his face turns into a scowl. Oh, this is good. He knows there's only one option, one person I can take.

"Who are you thinking about taking?" His tone is challenging. He already knows, but he wants me to say it. I have no problem saying her name at all. In fact, the more I say it, the better it sounds rolling off of my tongue.

"I don't know. Emmy?" I lift a brow right along with the corner of my lip.

"Nice. Two couples on a vacation on the beaches in Mexico with the white sand, the nude beaches, and I'm stuck here staring at fucking trees and shit. Fuckers," Jackson pouts.

"No fucking way!" he yells at me before he turns to put Jackson in his place. "And that's one fucking couple and another undercover woman and man working together."

"Lighten up, man. Your sister can handle it; it isn't any different than you dumping her in that house to stay with me. We'll just be sharing one room." I shrug like it's no big deal, which it isn't. I'll be focused on the mission of my life.

"A room with two beds," is Kaleb's reply. I don't have time for his crap right now, so I tell him what he wants to hear.

"Works for me. Someone make the call and get us rooms. Make sure they're suites while you're at it. Nothing but the best for the women." I think the asshole may have growled when I walked out right after I spoke to answer the vibrating phone in my pocket.

Yeah, he could never handle knowing what I've done with his sister. He'd lose his shit.

CHAPTER TWELVE

EMMY

I say good-bye to my mom and Jade at midnight. Though neither one of them knew the real reason why I kept glancing at the door waiting for my brother to come in, I could tell they both felt the edginess I've been feeling. I hope they suspect it had to do with the conversation I had earlier with him instead of the real reason I've spent the past two hours pretending I'm listening to Jade go on about finally setting a wedding date.

I'm ready to head back to the house and see with my own two eyes if Beau is really okay. I need to tell him I'm sorry for being pushy, even though I don't feel like I was; it's still the right thing to do after the way he reacted.

Then I'm going to go to bed and try my best to forget the fact he is most likely lying naked down the hall in bed with his smooth, hard chest, his tight abs, and a cock that was made to fuck on repeat.

Beau Harris would be like winning the grand prize of men. Sounds dumb, but it's the truth. From the little I know about the man, I can see how much he cares about those around him. I can tell he is a gives-more-than-he-takes kind of guy. And Jade, I feel for her. She's told me time and again how much she misses her friend, who she felt like she could talk to about anything. She's lost two friends in all of this, and I can see how hard this is on her.

She's told me how important he is to her and that he's always been there for her. That's a rarity in a man. It's a trait my brother has as well. Even if he's overbearing, the one thing I'll always know is he's there for me no matter what happens.

If only I knew Beau well enough to be able to guide him back to the man he was, I would do what I could. I'm not talking sexually. I'm talking the everyday living and laughing as he does something out of the norm that will make him notice he has a life yet to live. I know Mallory would not want him to become the bitter and angry man he is now. No one would want that for someone they love.

The sound of the front door opening draws my attention from the corner of the couch where I've been sitting for the past half hour. The room is dim with only the glow of the flat screen television shining on me and blocking my ability to see him in any way other than a silhouette.

"Hey," he says calmly then sits down on the opposite end of the couch.

God, he looks beat up. He has dark circles under his eyes and around the cuts from yesterday's fight. His hair is a mess and that scruff is begging me to run my hands over it.

"Jade filled me in a little. Are you doing okay?" Shit. Of course he isn't okay, you dipshit.

"Surprisingly, I am. I won't lie to anyone and say that reading all of that evidence didn't bring back the worst night of my life, because it sure as hell did. The thing is though, I feel good about it in a way that brings me some sort of peace, knowing we're taking off to investigate a strong hunch I have." This man beside me speaks so surely of himself; it's somewhat baffling and exciting at the same time to see this change in him.

The idea of him feeling peaceful is a reprieve to the hell that seeped out of his eyes a few hours ago. Physically, he seems more relaxed in the way he sits with his legs sprawled out on the coffee table in front of him. His arm is splayed across the back of the dark-blue couch, and his glare is now transfixed on me.

He may look exhausted, but he doesn't look defeated anymore. His shoulders are curled back, his head is higher, and as if it could be any more possible, the man is an absolute danger to my existence. I need to get away from him before I crawl on his lap, hike up my skirt, and ride his big cock.

"Well, I'm going to bed. I hope you get the answers you need." I reach across the couch and give his hand a gentle squeeze. Because, well, what else am I supposed to do? He's here, he's talking, and there really isn't anything left for me to say.

"I apologize, Emmy. I was an asshole. I should've never talked to you the way I did today." His words stop me right before I turn the corner to the hallway where I would disappear out of his sight. My back is to him, but I can hear and feel the sincerity in his voice. He means it.

"I accept your apology." My heart begins to flutter over a simple apology, which is something it never does. My head is scattered with all kinds of commotion pulling me in every direction. I'm usually composed and the one in charge, yet here I am ready to falter at the feet of a man who I wonder if he even knows what the hell he's doing to me.

This man has me all tied up in a knot. I don't get it at all. He's not damaged, yet he is. He's emotionally unavailable, yet he isn't. He's hurting, yet he's not.

"There's one more thing I need to tell you before you go to bed." I turn to meet his heated glare. His eyes roam up and down my bare legs, lingering at the center of my thighs. Yes, I'm teasing him in a way I shouldn't. Now that he notices I have no panties on underneath the thin material of this dress, and even though he has seen me naked and had his face buried deep in my pussy, I feel more exposed than I did earlier today.

"What is it?" I somehow manage to get those three little words out of my mouth without sounding like some schoolgirl with a stupid little crush.

"I told Kaleb I would tell you this. You and I are going with Jade and Kaleb to Mexico tomorrow. We have a lead and need your help with staying undercover and we just found out we leave in the morning. He's telling your mom now. He said if you needed him to give him a call. He'd be right here." My eyes go wide not so much from them needing my help, I would do anything to help them find out who's responsible for this.

It's going to Mexico that has those flutters stopping right along with my heart shrinking in my chest.

That's where Ty was. That's where they captured and tortured Kaleb. This can't be true. Kaleb told me everything and asked me to never tell our mother. Even though I swear at times the way she looks at Kaleb when he walks into her home and sees the photos of my good for nothing dead brother right alongside ours, she knows Kaleb's the one who ended Ty's life.

My mom would never admit her suspicions for the sake of the love she has for the son who has loved and respected her like any child should. She would never hurt him like that by making him admit to the horror. Kaleb will always live with some sort of regret, but this, this will eat away at him like the horrible memory it is.

I need to see him or at least talk with him to make sure he's okay. This will leave a bleeding wound that may never heal in my brother no matter how hard he tried to conceal it or tuck it way. Knowing that Ty had anything to do with this could break my brother again.

I'm thankful for the unconditional love Jade has for him and the strength she has to hold him together. I feel terrible all of a sudden thinking my brother may have had something to do with the tragedy that haunts Beau.

I feel sick. The enchiladas my mom made are rolling around in my stomach. Voices are screaming in my head, telling me this is not my fault, but a part of me knows it was my blood that may have done this to him.

"No," I whisper. "God, Beau. Please tell me the hunch along with the nasty taste in my mouth and the sinking feeling in the pit of my stomach is wrong." He says nothing, only a look of sympathy conveying back at me.

I've always considered myself to be a strong woman, one who is independent and carefree. I've always known exactly what I wanted to do with my life. I did my best to stay out of trouble until I left for college, staying focused on what I needed to do to become a doctor. If only I would have been able to stop my brother from leaving in the first place, then none of this would have happened.

"Emmy, stop. Right the fuck now. I know what the hell you're thinking, and there is no way I will let that shit consume your mind. I lived it for months, and as you know, it nearly drowned me. It's not anyone's fault that there are sick and twisted people out there. We can't control the actions of others. The only thing we can do is seek revenge and put an end to this fucked-up nightmare so we can all live. Listen," he tells me then moves quickly to stand in front of me.

He cups my face, and I let him by welcoming his warm hands as he tilts my head up to look into his crystal-clear eyes. I feel as if the tables are turning, where he's the one trying to heal me. It shouldn't be this way, and yet his touch, his gaze slices into me enough to halt my thoughts.

"I don't know what's happening between us. There's something. You feel it as much as I do. But," he swipes his thumb back and forth gently across my bottom lip, "what I know won't happen between the two of us is guilt. Not anymore for me and definitely never for you. Do you get me, Emmy? I need your strength. I'm not afraid to ask for it. Now, go call your brother. I think you need him more than you need me right now." I desperately want to tell him how sorry I am, but I can't seem to put together a coherent sentence. The guilt is still there, slowly drifting away behind the determination of those first words he spoke about something happening between the two of us. He has no idea how much I wanted to hear him acknowledge he feels it too, but if he's right about all of this and my brother had something to do with this, Kaleb is going to be devastated.

"Thank you," I whisper to his retreating back. He stops at the threshold of his doorway. His shoulders rise and fall in a brief contemplating measure before he turns and with long, unwavering strides and makes his way back to me. One hand slides around my waist, the other to the nape of my neck as he pulls me into his massive body, and I can feel hardness everywhere.

If there's one thing I do know about this man, it's that he takes what he wants. He gets what he needs and gives it right back. His lips clash against mine. He growls, his sound savaged, his mouth attacking, his lips biting, bruising, and sending a throbbing ache that starts at my core and stops at my chest.

He lifts me up by placing his hands on my bare ass, our mouths heated, and my fingers digging into his shoulders. I know what he's doing, he's reminding me that even though we are sleeping in separate beds tonight, that the desire he has for me is more than a fuck for him to get off on. He's right, there is something happening between us. Something that may take a while to figure out. Something I know with every swipe of my tongue across his that I want, but I'm not going to rush into anything with him, knowing how fragile he is right now.

One of his hands slaps my ass lightly, making me cry out into his mouth. God, I want him. He starts to walk me into my bedroom before he flicks on the light, never taking his mouth from mine. When our lips finally part and he places me down on my bed, his eyes are as untamed as that kiss was. He's dark and sinful right now, and looking at him, I can tell he feels just as alive as I do after that kiss. I'm not sure what to think, or what to say, or what even sparked him to kiss me like that.

"I gotta go before I take advantage of you again. I want nothing more than to fuck that tight pussy of yours again, and you have no idea where else my mind has gone while I carried you in here. Good night, Emmy."

CHAPTER THIRTEEN

HARRIS

The minute I saw her sitting on the couch, I knew without a doubt there is something about Emmy that has crawled under my skin. After the way I treated her today, she still sat there and waited for me to come back to the house just to see if I was alright. She's a saint in a sinful seductress body, and it tortures me to know she's getting to me.

I'm done denying that there isn't something between us. Whatever it is has given me a sense of hope, and that's all I have to hold on to right now. As fucked up as this life of mine is, if she's willing to hang on for the ride until we get to the bottom of this, then I'll do everything to get to know her better and see if we're compatible outside of this fucked-up situation.

As much as I want this to be over so that we can all live peacefully knowing the cocksuckers responsible suffer in a way they've never dreamed, I can't help but be happy to spend a few days with her and maybe get to know her better. She has a way of calming me, which is something I need right now.

My only problem is Kaleb. The man has had my back and pushed my limits through all of this. I care about the barbaric idiot and have no idea how he is going to handle this. I guess it's a talk I should probably have with him if we decide to continue whatever it is we have started.

By the time I've gone for a run and taken a long shower, my aching cock is still as hard as it was when I first noticed she was bare underneath that dress. I decide to throw caution to the wind and say the hell with it. Right or wrong, I need to fuck her. There hasn't been anything I've done right since I first noticed her here. I guess this means I may as well just dive in and do what I'm feeling. It's been six months since Mallory's death, and Emmy is the first woman I've been able to even look at.

I have an itch to go see her right now. I can't wait to spend some time with her in Mexico. I'm going to find out everything I can about what makes Emmy Maverick tick, right down to her sexual limits. And that's all going to start right now.

I make my way down the hall to her room, only to see her bent over, one leg on the bed, the other on the floor. That tempting ass is bare, and my cock twitches as I watch her move around, oblivious to the fact I'm watching.

"Don't move." She jumps to the sound of my voice. The hair from her ponytail whips as she turns to look at me. Her eyes go wide as she stares down at my hands inside my shorts. I'm already stroking my cock.

Her head tilts, and she licks her lips slowly in a way that would drive a sane man crazy and undoes me. Her lips are purely fuckable. There isn't a thing about her that isn't made to be fucked. Her hips make my hands ache to grip them while I imagine taking her from behind. My fingers itch to leave marks all over her tight ass. *Fuck me. That ass, that hair, her beautiful face.* I want it all. I let my shorts fall to the floor while my hand still strokes up and down my shaft, my eyes never leaving her naked body.

"I thought you said I needed my rest," she teases playfully.

"I changed my mind. You'll need the rest alright, after I've exhausted your body like it's never been exhausted before. I've been hard since I saw you weren't wearing any underwear. It got harder when I held your ass in the palm of my hands, and I'm harder now that your sweet ass is taunting me to take it." Her reaction shows me she's all in when her brows raise and the sweetest yet dirtiest smile spreads across those unforgettable lips. *Fuck. I'm going to be screwed in more ways than one.*

"Well, what are you waiting for then?" She wiggles her ass, places her other leg on the bed, hands in front of her, and fuck me, there isn't a better sight than seeing her submit to me like she is right now. I grip ahold of her hair and pull it back in my fist. I take my other hand and grip my cock, sliding over the crack of her luscious ass and then down to where the tip hits her wetness and back up again.

I bend over her and take her mouth as she looks back at me. Tasting her lips only makes me crazier. The noises this sexy little soon-to-be doctor makes drive me mad. Half pain, half pleasure whimpers into my mouth as I yank and tug on her hair. My dick is coated with her wetness, making it easy to slide into her a few times.

My fingers slide into her heat, coating that sweet smell of her arousal all over them. When she clamps down on them, I pull her hair to the brink of where it has to be painful for her. All I can think about is making her feel me, watching her fall apart as I fuck her over and over. I want to watch her explode.

Her gasps and moans as I thrust into her, then slide out to coat the rim of her ass are all I need to realize this woman has a kinky side to her that I'm going to take advantage of. Not in the way of using her; in the way of watching her come undone below me. I want to watch her spiral out of control and fuck her until her legs give out from the pleasure I'm giving her.

"Fuck. You are so damn beautiful," I tell her then take my finger and dip it into her ass. I continue from her pussy to her ass, making sure she is lubed up enough to take me. She's on the verge of coming with every stroke of my finger inside of her.

"So are you," she tells me with breath so ragged she can barely get the words out. She arches back even more; she's so damn flexible, perfect, and barely able to talk. I have her in a daze. A fog of sexual need. Just the way I want her.

"If I hurt you, you tell me."

"Okay," she pants as her eyes flutter closed.

"You sure you can handle this?" I want her to know I won't purposely do a thing to hurt her.

"Just fuck me already. I'm on the edge here, Beau." Her left hand lifts, and I lose sight of it, but I feel it when she toys with her clit, every once in a while touching the underside of my dick.

"Holy fuck. You're sexy as hell. I want you to scream when you come." I mean what I say. She better let go. That ass better be slamming back onto my cock as she rides out as many orgasms as I can get out of her.

I take a slight step back to line my cock up, but first I slap both of her ass cheeks. The sound of my hand cracking across her porcelain skin bounces off the walls. I wait a moment until her skin starts to turn pink before I do anything else, making me harder than I was earlier.

"You love it rough, don't you?" Her body jolts forward slightly only for me to jerk it right back to where I need her to be. Her ass is tight and warm as I push against the pressure it's giving me.

"Yes, I love it rough and hard," is all she yells out the farther I go. Good answer, I want to say, but my brain won't function, because damn, this feels so incredible. I have no words right now to form a coherent sentence.

Her back arches, her ass grips me, and once I've sunk in until my balls are ready to explode, I still myself for one second before I lose control. I need to be gentle at first, not domineering like my mind wants me to be. I start to move slowly, whispering how fucking good she feels into her ear.

Even though my hands are itching to hold onto her hair, I let it go so she can be as comfortable as she can get. She grinds her ass against me, and I drive into her once again.

Once she starts to move on me even faster, I decide to take over. My hands grip her hips hard enough to leave marks as my cock drives forward and we fuck. Hard. Fast. And intense.

"Ahhh," she cries out. I have no idea how her ass feels tighter when she comes, but it does. It pulls my release to the head of my cock. I'm ready to come so hard that I strain with everything I have not to let go.

"I need one more out of you, Emmy. Finger yourself." I slap her ass again. She jars forward, and I swear like a motherfucker my dick can feel her fingers fucking herself furiously up against the walls of her ass.

"Jesus, Beau. I never thought this would feel so good." Her voice is laced with desire.

"Me either, Emmy. I'm not sure what the hell you are doing to me."

A few more hard thrusts, and I'm losing it right along with her, her name falling from my lips at the same time she cries out mine.

I pull out slowly, allowing her body to relax on the bed. Her breathing is so rapid I can see her pulse through the skin on the side of her neck when she turns and gazes up at me.

"You alright?" She smirks at my comment. In fact, the crazy woman goes into a full-on laugh. I haven't heard anything as beautiful as the sound of her laughter in a long time. It catches me off guard.

"And here I thought you were an asshole," she says through her little fit.

"Taking that ass of yours is what made you decide I wasn't?" I bend down and tug on my shorts as I wait for her response.

"No. A real asshole wouldn't make sure a woman is alright after what we did." I exhale. She is alright. In fact, she's much better than alright.

"Don't count me out yet, Emmy. I meant what I said about hanging in there with me. Let's take this slow, get to know each other in Mexico with any free time we may have. If you can do that, I'll prove to you I'm a dick, not an asshole." She simply shrugs at my sarcasm instead of laughing at me this time. She's hesitant, and I get that. I mean, hell, one minute I think I know what I'm doing, the next I have no goddamn clue.

"I'm not going anywhere except to the bathroom to clean up." Her tone is playful yet still guarded. I'll take it and leave it at that. I do what any man would do; I help her out of her bed then watch her sway into the bathroom tugging her hair out of her ponytail. *Good*, I think to myself when I see it cascade down her back. *I'm not going anywhere either, Emmy.*

"Shit," I mumble when I roll over and look at the clock that reads 8 AM. I haven't slept this good in months. No nightmares. Nothing. I stretch and look over to where Emmy should be, except she isn't there. Then the smell of bacon assaults my nose. Good, I'm starving.

Climbing out of bed, I stumble down the hall to my room, take a piss, brush my teeth, and snag my phone. I need to call my mom to let her know we possibly have a lead and I'll be leaving for a while. She's been good about giving me the space I need even though I can sense how worried she is about me whenever we talk.

"Hey, Mom," I say when she answers.

"Son. I was thinking about calling you this morning." Her tone tells me she's happy to hear from me. God, I love her like no other. The sacrifices she's made for me are unbelievable. This lady has dedicated her life to making mine a happy one.

I walk into the living room and whisper, "My mom," to Emmy when she turns around to the sound of my voice. I can't help but stare at the way she looks with her hair still wet. Her shorts are clinging to her ass, and she has a tight red t-shirt on. She must've showered, which makes me realize how hard and peacefully I slept.

My mom says something to me at the exact time Emmy holds up a mug and points to the coffee pot. I nod and continue to carry on my conversation with her, telling her everything I can about the mission, which isn't much. Of course, she expresses her concern like the good mom she is.

By the time we hang up with me promising her I'll call her the first chance I get, she's pissing and moaning that Vice will be hanging around a little longer for her protection. Emmy has a plate of bacon, eggs, and toast on the table for me when I end the call, and I can't help but look at her in a new way this morning.

"Did you talk to Kaleb about Mexico? We can't have you going into this feeling guilty," I ask her then dig into my food. It tastes damn good. You don't realize how badly you mistreat your body by only eating enough to get by when you're barely living.

"I did. It's human nature to feel that way. Just like Kaleb, I will always tell myself that maybe if I'd tried just a little harder, then Ty wouldn't have been so fucked up in his head, that he would still be here, that we could be as close as Kaleb and I are, and that my mom could have her son back. And, of course, innocent people would be alive." Her eyes drag up to mine as if she realizes she shouldn't have said the last part. It's a subject I'm not ready to touch on with her. I may never be able to. There's not a chance in hell I will let her take the blame for this.

"I told you last night just like I'm sure Kaleb told you. That shit is not your fault. Ty was your brother. You didn't make the choices he made for him. I'll respect you and your mother for that. Deal?" I shovel the last few bites into my mouth, get up, and take my plate to the sink before I grab another cup of coffee and go to her.

"Come here." I don't bother waiting for her to stand. I lift her out of her chair with a gentle tug on her hand and pull her into my arms. A woman deserves to be respected, cherished, and made to feel good. It may not have seemed like I treated her that way when I went into her room last night, but the one thing I do know about her is, she's as stubborn as her brother.

Yet, she's a lady, and they seem to take things more personally than men do. She needs to get over that right now.

"What was that for?" She draws back to look at the sincerity I'm giving her with my eyes. My words that follow need to sink into her. I'm sure as I'm standing here she's heard the same thing earlier when talking to Kaleb.

"Where we're going is dangerous. We have no idea what the hell we are going to discover down there. I'm assuming you know we're going down there to talk to a woman named Samantha Williams, who dated Ty for three years?"

"Yes. Kaleb told me." Emmy gives me a quizzical look.

"It's all we have to go on at this point, and since she seems to be someone we'll be able to make contact with, I'm hoping like hell she'll be willing to talk to us. We need to know everything she knew about Ty. You need to push all that shit out of your mind and focus on what we need to do. And that is to help us find out who in the fuck Ty had helping him. That's where you and Jade come in. We know very little about her. Her father owns the resort we'll be staying at. I want to know why a man as powerful as Ty was down there let a woman walk away from him. If she did it by choice or was forced to. No guilt, no fear, Emmy. You need to be strong, show her and anyone else we come in contact with that you are determined, demanding, and a woman who will not take bullshit answers. People will pick up on every weak emotion. This is out of your league, and I get that, but I need you to help me stay undercover. Do you understand?"

I hate to sound like the asshole she's called me many times. She needs to have this drilled in her head. The tough Emmy needs to come back. The woman who gave me shit the first time I met her needs to show her horns, dig her claws in, and follow Jade's lead when they talk to this chick.

"Like I told Kaleb, I may not know what you all do and how you do it, but this means as much to me as all of you." Her response is exactly what I need to hear. She wouldn't be going if we didn't think she could take this on.

"I'm reminding you this is not a vacation for any of us. We could be walking into some serious shit down there. Now, go pack."

CHAPTER FOURTEEN

EMMY

"You do not let my mom out of your sight." I stand alongside Jade and Beau with my carry-on bag in my hand, listening to Kaleb bark out orders to Jackson and Steele like he's a drill sergeant. My eyes internally roll at the way he commands them to do this and that and everything in between. I wait for a smartass remark to come from that non-filtered mouth of Jackson's, but when all he does is squeeze my brother's shoulder, I know this is real, serious, and dangerous.

Am I scared? Hell, yes. Am I determined to get to the bottom of this, to help in any way I can? You bet the sweet ass of the man standing next to me I am. I hear Kaleb bellow out a few more orders and try to hold my tongue. He wouldn't be leaving her if he didn't trust them, so why is he talking to them like they have no idea what the hell to do?

Kaleb may be the leader of the group, but these guys are a team. They have each other's back, and now we're both leaving them with the only parent we've had.

"Kaleb, go. I'll be fine with these guys." My mom gives him a hug and then moves to pull me into her arms. She's shaking. I can feel how nervous she is about the two of us going together. The three of us have always looked out for one another. I feel horrible for leaving her. I'm not going to tell her that though. She's our mother; she'll worry no matter what I say.

Beau takes my bag from the ground where I sat it when Mom wraps her arms around me. He walks to the back of the SUV and places it inside while Mom whispers in my ear to please be careful. I give her a tight smile along with a kiss on the cheek, while the words Beau spoke this morning sit firmly in the front of my brain.

Show no fear. So I don't and I won't. "Love you, Mom," I say then step into the open door, climbing into the back next to Jade, who looks cool and collected.

I'm nervous more than I'm scared. Nervous of what we may find down there. Worried that Ty had his hands in Mallory's death. Even though both of these men who are now talking strategy in the front seat tried to reassure me I shouldn't feel this way, I do. I always will.

At least doing this and the way Beau tried to pull that guilt out of my system last night with his words of encouragement, leave me with more hope since I first learned that Ty possibly had his hands in this.

I watch the interaction between the two men in the front. They genuinely care about one another as they go over a few details of how this is all going to go down. Even though the sexy man who I can't seem to take my eyes off of has blatantly told me his heart is closed up, I'm proud of how far he's come in a matter of days. If I stop and think about it, his heart may be closed off to a relationship, but it's genuine. I know this about him. If he were as shallow as he makes himself out to be, he would hate both Kaleb and me, blame us for Ty's actions. People do that when they grieve or they're hurt. They strike out and blame others. The man I met a few days ago may have done that, but not the man here today. Whether he wants to admit it or not, he's healing.

"This chick better talk," I hear Beau say, bringing me back to the conversation I should be paying attention to.

"If she doesn't, I'll do what needs to be done to make her. You two need to let me handle it. Remember that," Jade pronounces from her seat beside me. I swallow back those nerves so no one can see they are crawling up my throat and squeezing off my air supply.

Good God, I hope she talks. I hope she makes it easy on everyone and tells us everything she knows. Gives us a hint or some kind of name or anything to get this over with so we can capture that killer. Beau needs to move on with his life, and he can't if there's no closure in this. I feel like a bitch thinking that way. Life will never be the same no matter what, even if the person behind this ends up in a body bag.

Both Jade and Kaleb explained it all to me this morning when we talked. I'm here posing as Beau's girlfriend, which is far from the truth. At least in his eyes. He's tried to make it perfectly clear he's using me. For the most part, he is, except I catch him looking at me when he doesn't think I'm watching.

I know when a person is attracted to someone more than sexually. I also get the fact he's afraid. I would be too if I were him. I squirm in my seat thinking about last night and the way he took control. I let him come right into my room and fuck me in the ass. I'd do it again, because nothing has felt as good as being screwed by a man who takes what he wants and still whispers in your ear asking you if you're alright. A man who's only out for himself would not give a shit. He's fooling no one but himself. But hey, I'll let him continue to do so, even if it means he walks away from me for good when this is all over.

"Hey. You need to quit overthinking. With my experience and your kind bedside manner, we got this. Like I told you earlier, there has to be a reason why she left him and why he let her go without harming her. You'll do great, Emmy." If Jade only knew that wasn't what I was thinking, she'd be ready to strangle me. I do revel in Jade's words and her confidence she has in me though.

The thing is, these three are trained for this kind of shit. I may have the proper etiquette of a doctor and I sure as hell haven't had to sit down with someone yet and show my concern or tell them I'll do everything I can to help them, but I will. I'll do whatever I can to help them solve this. Plus, this is personal.

"I'm not overthinking. I'm planning my own ways to get her to talk. You three are intimidating as hell. It might be best if I talk to her myself. Like I said, I'll do anything I can to help." Jade grins beside me and tosses me a smug smirk, while Kaleb shouts from the front seat.

"You let Jade lead, Emmy. We know very little about this woman. We're stepping into her territory, blindsiding her.

It may appear she hasn't talked to Ty in years before he died, that doesn't mean she hasn't. She could be in on this for all we know. Jade can handle it if she refuses to talk."

"For fuck's sake, Kaleb, I'm not scared. Give me some damn credit here!" I yell back, then turn to watch Jade kick the back of his seat, which gets her a glare from him through the rearview mirror.

"Shut it, Kaleb. She's not an idiot." I start laughing as Jade hands my brother his ass for a few seconds.

"No, she isn't, but she is my baby sister and she doesn't know how this works."

"Well, I can guarantee I'll get more out of her than you ever would. You need to lighten up, relax a bit, for crying out loud. I grew up with dealing with your bossy ass, didn't I? Shall we tell them how many times I got you to tell me something? Like all the times I bribed you to do something for me when I would catch you sneaking out of the house or coming home drunk?" This little secret gets him to lighten his mood instantly. It also gets the four of us laughing our asses off all the way to the airport, where we board the plane.

We get to sit in first class and pretend to be vacationing. Our acting starts the second we leave the vehicle.

"Wow. This place is beautiful." I loop my arm through Beau's and pretend to be his girlfriend as we walk through the sliding doors of 'The All Inclusive Casa Vallarta Beach Resort in Puerto Vallarta'. In the real world, this would be amazing if we were really coming here for a vacation as a couple, but I can already tell we'll enjoy this.

The plane ride convinced me again that what we have going on is nothing more than purely fucking. He read through papers, instructed me on what to do and say, purely professional, and it sucked not to be able to touch him like I wanted to.

He's given me the best fucks of my life, but he's made it perfectly clear that's all it is just a bit ago. So I swallow the feelings I have and take in the reception area.

Everything is wide open. You can smell and see the ocean through the walkway I notice in the distance. The warm breeze and palm trees make a great scenery for the people milling about, draped in bathing suits and money. This place screams luxury, and it really is a shame we can't explore it more.

"Well, fuck me." Both Kaleb and Beau approach us with our keycards in their hands and scowls on their faces.

"What's wrong?" Jade places her arm on Kaleb's lovingly. Her touch alone calms him before he gets any louder than he already is. I look around, catching a snooty, upturned nose from some high-class bimbo in high heels and a bikini. Dumb bitch. I hope she trips and falls on her flat ass. I crane my head back around in time to hear my brother say, "I asked if I could set up a meeting to speak with Samantha. Apparently, she's at the grand opening of another one of their resorts. She won't be back for a few days," he tells Jade as I listen. I watch Beau's reaction. He looks frustrated. I see his pain all over his face, while my mind musters up something quick to say to try and get the two of them to relax. The exact words I was thinking flow out of Jade's mouth.

"Well then, we have two days to take advantage of this beautiful place. Let's have some fun. All of us could use it." Her hand glides from his arm to his chest. The way he looks at her with love and adoration makes me happy for my brother that he's finally found someone who is similar to him in so many ways, yet can calm him with a few words and a simple touch.

"Yeah. We have no choice. I'm not leaving here until we speak to her," he replies.

"Let's get settled in our rooms then. We can meet you two back here in a few hours." Jade turns to me to get my intake.

"Sure. I'm going to unpack and walk around. It's been years since I've been anywhere," I tell them all.

"Don't go by yourself." Kaleb tries to toss out his demands at me.

"We're in a gated all-inclusive resort, Kaleb. There are people everywhere. I'm not leaving the place. Now, go and don't feel like any of you have to entertain me. I can drink, lie on the beach, and do whatever I want."

"Don't go to the topless beach without me." Jade laughs as they walk away, leaving the two of us standing there uncomfortably.

"Let's go check out the room. I'll change and leave you alone." I have no clue if he wants to be alone or not. I don't blame him for being as distant as he has been. I'm sure some of it was a front for Kaleb and Jade so they won't suspect he's been fucking my brains out. I mean that literally. He's all I can think about. But here, where he needs to remain focused, I'll give him all the space he needs.

"Follow me," he says dryly.

I slowly follow him through the lush green foliage with the most beautiful red flowers I've ever seen. The girls in skimpy bathing suits and jewels watch Beau as he passes. I should feel oddly out of place with my white gauze, short spaghetti strap dress and my white flip-flops while these women parade around in barely anything at all, but I don't.

Beau stops briefly in front of a pond full of a variety of colorful fish. "Pretty fucking cool place," is all he says and then continues on until we stop in front of our small little private villa with its private deck with two wicker chairs and a table.

He opens the door with a swipe of his card, turns, and hands me one, then pushes the door open, allowing me to enter first. I feel the tension rolling off of him, crashing all over me. I'm not going to ask him what his problem is or if I've done something wrong. I know what's troubling him. He has to pretend we're something we will never be.

"Jesus, when I asked for a suite I was fucking joking," he bellows out from behind me. My eyes are wide as I take a look at the open floor plan in front of me.

There's a small kitchenette off to the side and a giant living room with red and white matching furniture. A black table with a magazine and a basket full of fruit and a bottle of wine sitting in the middle of the room make it feel very modern. I move past it all and head straight for the bedroom, where I can see the ocean from the set of sliding glass doors.

"Oh my," I say too quietly. I have no clue if he followed me or not. There's a king-sized bed up against the wall with a red and white comforter. The walls are painted the same soft color of gold as the living area. This place is breathtaking.

I slide the door open, inhaling the minute my feet hit the tile, and rest my hands on the ledge. There's a small walkway that leads to the white sandy beach. People are in the crystal-clear water, and I can see many of them sun-bathing topless.

I hear his footsteps behind me and notice his face drop when he sees the beach. He lowers his sunglasses, and I watch him look at two women with perfect tits as they pass. "I'm getting my bottoms on and going out to chill on the beach." I throw my bag on the bed before I unzip it and begin to dig for my favorite turquoise string bikini.

"The fuck you are." His loud response surprises me, and I let my eyes scan his face before I continue to search through my bag. *Whatever, buddy!*

"Beau, you're not going to tell me what I can and can't do." I pull on the strings of my bathing suit until both pieces come out and turn my back on him as I start to walk to change in the bathroom. He meets me at the door, grabs me by my waist, and pulls me against him just as my hand reaches out in search of the light switch.

"You'll be wearing your fucking bathing suit at all times, or I'll drag your ass in here kicking and screaming without a care in the damn world. Remember, your brother is here and doesn't need to see you on display, not to mention all the fucking perverts out there wanting an eyeful of ass and tits." Releasing me, he politely holds the door open with the palm of his hand. He wants me to obey him and walk through the door, but instead, I spin around and give him a piece of my mind.

"Here's the deal. You learn not to be so damn bossy, and then maybe I'll listen to whatever you have to say." I wanted to say more, but he stops me mid-sentence. His lips land on mine, and he forces me against the wall with his weight. He leans into me, running his hands roughly over my skin until he has silenced me, and he knows it. It's like the fight in me just disappeared without a trace. I'm surrendering to this contradictive man.

"If you walk around without your top, I'm going to walk around naked. Take that in and suck on it. My dick is always hard around you, so you know I'll be sporting a big cock for the world to see when you're near." I'm irritated now. Surely, I don't want another woman seeing his glorious package. I bite my tongue and stand strong with my retort.

"Try it. It's a topless beach, not a nude beach. And I'll ignore the sucking comment, thank you very much." I'd probably do more than suck on it if he were to whip it out right now.

"Actually, it's a nude beach, but we won't be joining in on those festivities." He frustrates me with his demands, but I get it. I'd wind up in a Mexican jail for choking anyone who looks his way or for public indecency if he were to strip down himself.

"If you promise me you'll go skinny dipping in the ocean one night, then I'll agree to your ridiculous demands." He smiles like he's looking forward to that, and in all honesty, it sounds much better to me anyway.

"This trip may be the death of my dick if you keep it up. Now, strip down and let me watch you slide those strings over your body. I want a picture in my head of what you look like underneath it as I watch you on the beach." I move slowly, teasing him as I shimmy out of every article of clothing I have on. He watches with a hungry look in his eyes, making me feel more confident than I ever have in my life.

The very second I've discarded my panties, he's back to rubbing up against me. He's already hard and lifting me up into his hard body. "I'm about to fuck you in Mexico." His voice is deep and so damn sexy. His lips land on mine just as he finishes speaking, my mouth opening willingly to seek out his tongue.

He lays me down softly, but aggressively works his way over my body. I welcome the roughness of his touch and love how he seems to be even more so with me in every aspect than he was back at the compound. Maybe coming to Mexico was exactly what he needed. Honestly, I was worried it would cause him to go into a tailspin and would ruin any bit of healing he's managed in the past few days.

He grabs a handful of my hair, pulling just perfectly, causing me to gasp into his mouth. Reaching between us, he releases the button on his shorts, sliding them down far enough to slide into me.

"Yes. So tight." He speaks with each thrust, telling me how good we feel together, and I accept every word he says, agreeing and begging for more.

He moves fast and hard, his body pounding me into the mattress. The bed squeaks loudly, but neither one of us care at all. The beach goers no doubt will be able to hear us, and it isn't until he covers my mouth that I even consider how loud I was being myself.

"Fuck. You're so deep," I mumble through his hand. It doesn't take many words from me before he's pulling out and squirting his release all over my stomach.

"Maverick will be here soon. You'd better be dressed. I'm going to put my bags by the couch. He doesn't need to know I was just balls deep in his baby sister while we're on a mission."

CHAPTER FIFTEEN

HARRIS

I'm out of my fucking mind. I can't believe I'm here in Mexico, and the first thing I do is bury my cock deep inside Emmy, knowing Maverick is on the other side of that wall. He's going to come in here with a gun and try to shoot my dick off for that.

I hear a knock on the door before I'm finished pulling my shirt back on. Emmy rushes to the bathroom, and I pull the doors closed to the bedroom, hoping if it is Maverick that he won't be completely nosy. He's not stupid. My guess is he's figured it out or he's about to.

Opening the door quickly, I startle Jade, causing her to jump. She's dressed in a bikini, and I look at Maverick, who's scowling behind her. I can see he's just as unhappy about this beach thing as I am.

Either that, or he heard how loud we were. How good I told her she felt. It wouldn't be a lie, that's for damn sure. There's something about her that drives me crazy.

I wonder if Jade has threatened him as well with going topless. I need to remember not to react around him if Emmy comes out here mouthing off about it, or he'll pick up on this shit from a mile away.

"You fucking my sister? Because I swear we just heard screaming coming from this room." Holy fuck. I don't even know how to respond to that, but I start laughing, because apparently, that's what I do when I'm nervous.

"Kaleb. Don't you dare come in here and start accusing us when you know damn well we're both grown ass adults." Emmy barrels through the sliding doors, and I just step back. Jade's eyes meet mine, and her smile turns into a full-on amused look with a hint of worry rather quickly.

"I was just joking, but by the looks of it, I may have just hit the nail on the fucking head." Maverick steps back against the stucco wall across from our room and runs his hand through his hair. "Not even an hour into Mexico, and I get shit like this dropped on me. How long has this been going on? Or did you just hit these doors and can't keep your fucking hands off of each other all of a sudden?" Jesus, he needs to calm the hell down. I may be nervous about him finding out, but he can stop talking so that everyone else around here doesn't know our business.

I open my mouth, ready to speak my peace, when Emmy begins to talk again. "We've been fucking for days. Don't worry your pretty little head, big brother. I'm not stupid thinking this is anything more than just that." Hearing her say that doesn't make me feel any better. It actually makes me feel a hundred times worse. *Well, you haven't told her any different, you asshole.* I haven't either. In fact, it's a topic we should discuss again.

Emmy walks into the small kitchenette, while Maverick's eyes bore into me. I shove my mental note aside as Jade stands between us and I can feel his urge to strangle me from across the doorway.

"Kaleb, get in here." Jade sticks her hand out for him to take. He doesn't take it, just strolls right in and stands in his usual arms folded over his chest position. I wait until the door catches and shuts behind me before I say what I need to.

"Don't worry. She's in good hands." I try to reassure him with my intentions, but before I can even try to convince myself, I stop talking. What am I going to say? This is more than just fucking for me? I love her? She completes me? No. None of that is true, and the truth of it is, this is just hard fucking with no hopes of being anything more, because I gave everything to Mallory. Emmy knows it. I know it. There really isn't room for discussing it further.

Fuck. I have no idea what the hell I'm doing when it comes to whatever this is between Emmy and me anymore.

"Did you know about this, Jade? Is that why you insisted they share this suite?" His focus shifts to Jade only for a second before returning to me.

"Kaleb. We had to pretend we're couples. You know that. This trip is going to be fun for us the first few days. You know we all need this, and if the two of them want to play around, who are we to say one word about it?"

"I'm her brother and his fucking boss. I know what he's doing, and I don't have to fucking agree with it." At least he knows what the fuck I'm doing. I sure as hell don't.

"No, you don't, but you can't stop them." Jade turns toward Kaleb when Emmy walks back into the room, going straight for her brother.

"You won't say a damn word about this. You'll accept whatever we decide to do and understand that I'm old enough to take care of myself." She points her finger in his face.

"He's grieving, Emmy," he gently tells her. In that instant, I feel like the asshole I look like, a man using a woman to get off while his heart is still attached to another. A woman I will never have again, see again, or hold again.

"We've talked a lot about all of that, and in some way we're helping each other through a tough time. Please, just let us do what feels right for us and don't interfere." He looks over her head at me before he lowers his lips to her forehead.

"You know I always have your back, and this will be no different. You just have to give me a minute to absorb it all. I came in joking and had no idea I was walking into something like this. And what kind of tough time are you having? Is it school?" The look on his face as he glares at me with eyes that basically say I'm a goddamn fool tells me we'll be talking soon, but that's understandable.

I remember how I felt when he came in all domineering with Jade. He needed to prove he deserves her, and he proved it over and over. That's something I'm afraid I can't say about myself. Mallory is still where my heart is, and after I have sex with Emmy, a part of me wishes like hell it was her in my arms and beneath me, sending noise into the neighbor's ears, but that will never happen. But I can't help but feel when I'm with Emmy, and that's something I've missed.

"No, Kaleb, school is fine. It just blurted out of my mouth that way. Can we drop it now, go to the beach, where Jade and I can work on our tans a little?" I restrain from watching Emmy walk out of the living room area and into the bedroom and reach for my suitcase. I pull out my swim shorts and grab hold of my suitcase. Deciding to throw caution to the wind, I join her in our bedroom to get ready. I may as well let Maverick know we plan to sleep in the same room this entire trip.

"Did that shit really have to go down the first day of the trip? Now he's going to be glaring at us both the entire time." I drop my clothes and pull on my board shorts before she starts to answers me.

"He'll get over it. Just give him a day or so, and we'll win him over with the idea of it. It's supposed to be a relaxing few days, and we all need that before we dive into the real reason we came. I'll remind him of that again if I need to." Emmy seems so strong and collected when it comes to Maverick. She actually reminds me a lot of Jade, which is why I probably get along well with her. Hell, it's probably why Kaleb was so interested in Jade.

"I guess if he doesn't and I find my death after all of this, at least I'll know it was for a woman. I can't think of a worthier cause." Her lips are shiny and just begging for me to touch

them one last time before I have to stay away. I lean forward
to kiss her, only to have her pull away.

"Okay, okay. Let's not push him. He does have a short
fuse, and we don't need to rub it in his face just yet." She
pushes against my chest, and I have to agree with her, for now
anyway.

"Let's do this beach thing. But for fuck's sake, you'd
better keep everything covered, or I'm stripping too. You'll
have a hard dick chasing you on the beach." Her laughter is
louder and sweeter than I expected to hear.

"Alright. I promise. Now, stop teasing me, or he'll really
hate the idea of us." She grabs my hand and leads me out of
the bedroom and into the room where I can still feel the
tension.

"We can get to the beach through our bedroom, if you'd
like," she tells the two of them. Jade's standing there with a
smile glued to her face, while Kaleb, well, his look may be one
that wants to permanently put me in the ground. I toss him a
look that says 'I'm ready to get this talk over with as soon as
you are,' and he nods back to me.

Emmy doesn't help the situation when she grabs
Jade's hand, the two of them leading the way through our
room, proving the messed-up bedding is a real thing. By the
growl coming from behind me, Kaleb knows it too.

What the fuck ever. I'm ready for this talk whenever he
is. The sooner the better. Like I said to myself earlier, our
situation may be entirely different than the way he was when

he first demanded I keep my distance from Jade. I'm fucked up, I'll admit it to anyone, but he will not interfere with this.

We make it past the deck and gated entry to our private little bungalow, then we're surrounded by beach and naked bodies, but even more so the sound of water rushing up the beach. The sun will be setting soon, and it shines very proudly across the water.

"It's breathtaking." Emmy sounds amazed by the view, and in all the times I've watched her, seeing her take all of this in makes me smile. She's obviously never seen anything like it, and even though I've been all over the world, this would be listed as one of the most captivating scenic memories to date.

"Let's set our stuff here," Jade proclaims after we walk down a small wooden bridge that leads to the sandy beach. The beach is crowded as fuck. I feel my heart thunder in my chest as I take them all in. It's been a long time since I've been around people other than at the compound, but I'll be damned the minute I look around seeing the happy couples I feel better. Although some of them are naked with their junk hanging out, a few with sculpted bodies, while most aren't, others are covered up in everything from scraps that barely cover their bodies to fully clothed. I find it doesn't bother me seeing how carefree they are. How easily they mill about like they should be. Happy, in love, and having a damn good time.

"Don't you have to rent these things or something?" Emmy asks, then unties some see-through thing from around her waist I never knew she put on.

"If you would have read the brochures in the room that stated these are reserved for guest of the hotel on a first come, first served basis and instead of heading straight for the bed, maybe you would have noticed." Kaleb scowls at me as he responds to Emmy. Yeah, our talk needs to happen now, or this sour puss with his forehead all crinkled is going to fucking blow.

I direct my head toward the water when Jade looks my way, hoping she gets the hint to take Emmy down there. She nods, then closes her mouth that was ready to strike out at Kaleb. Emmy on the other hand says, "I love you, Kaleb, but one more goddamn remark like that and I will knock you on your ass. Come on, Jade. I need a drink, my toes in the sand, and a walk." We both watch them walk away. The minute they're out of our earshot, I let out a laugh I didn't even know I was holding in.

"I'm not sure why you're laughing, you asshole." He folds his arms over his chest as if he's supposed to be intimidating me.

I shrug before I speak and sit down at the end of one of the lounge chairs and tell him like it is. "Listen, Kaleb. I get the need for you to want to protect her; in fact, I'd think less of you if you didn't. I won't lie to you either, man, she knows where my head's at and I've made sure to be upfront and honest about what I can be. She also realizes I'm not sure I can give her what she deserves. Emmy's a good woman. I can tell she wants more from me than what my heart is willing to give her right now. Don't be a dick and ruin the few days we have to have fun. Who the hell knows what kind of shit storm is in store for us when we talk to this woman. Let it go for now." He stands there watching the two of them as do I as they walk from the bar with a fruity cocktail in their hand, not looking our way once as they head straight for the water.

"It's easy for you to sit there and tell me that, Harris. She's my sister. Once this is over, I'll be the one picking her broken heart up off the ground if she falls for you. Not you. Not Jade. Me." He points at his chest. "On top of all that, we work together. I need you on this team. You fuck her over, and I don't give a shit how good you are, you'll be gone." I want to tell him that's bullshit. She won't be hurt and she'll go back to school where she'll find a man who appreciates her and forget about me. I can't though. He knows it.

As far as my place on this team, it's a risk I'm going to take. I sit there letting his words soak in before I say anything more. We watch her walk right into the water with no fear as the waves crash into her, making her giggle. She's far enough away to where I can't hear her laugh, but in my mind I can. That's when it hits me like a solid brick to the head. She's the first person who has drawn a laugh out of me since my life fell apart. The first person I've wanted to spend time with. And honest to fucking God, the first woman that after hearing those words from Kaleb, I would give anything to not have her heart crumble to the floor for the simple fact I would much rather keep it beating in her chest and a smile on her face.

"Give me time, brother. I need time to get to know her and time to figure this whole thing out. I'm not the type of guy to dump her on your doorstep and say, 'Here you go, clean up my mess.' I like her, and that's all I can give you until I find out who stole my soul from me. Until then, I don't have one to give to her or anyone." I glare up at him, taken aback by the strange look on his face as he's standing there staring down at me.

What the hell kind of look is that? He sits and lowers his head. I feel his pain for me and this whole fucked-up situation. It's fucked up, all of it. From to the reason we're all here right down to the fact I'm sitting here telling a brother I may or may not be using his sister for sex. I half expected him to go off on me and try to beat my ass. I sure as hell can't blame him if he takes a swing at me right now. He doesn't though. He exhales, lifts his head, and looks at me.

"You know what I think?" He lifts both of his brows, while one corner of his mouth quirks up in some fucked-up, cocky lift.

"Not really." I challenge him. It doesn't matter if I don't want to hear what he has to say or not. He's as stubborn and bullheaded as I am, the type of guy who says whatever the hell he wants to say whether you want to hear it or not.

"Tough shit, fucker. I saw the way you were watching her just now. You can't keep your eyes off of her. In the past few minutes, you told me you didn't have a soul. A man with no soul would not be sitting here with an older brother trying to convince him to give him time. He would say, 'Fuck you, Maverick.' So here's my take on you not having a soul. I think my sister is good for you. You may have started off by using her, but you're full of shit if you think you're trying to tell me you're only using her now."

CHAPTER SIXTEEN

EMMY

"Are you going to tell me what's going on between you two?" Jade snaps her fingers in my face, drawing my attention away from Kaleb and Beau. I can see from where we're standing at the beachfront bar that they're talking. Beau is sitting, while my brother is staring out into the water. His stiff shoulders are unyielding. If he starts a fight, I swear I will knee him in his crotch and try to drop him to the ground. I haven't done it in years, but I won't hesitate to try. He wouldn't fight me on it anyway. He never did.

"We're fucking," I tell her truthfully.

"Well, no shit. What I want to know is where your head is in this, Emmy. He's messed up. I don't want to see you get hurt." Her hand gestures toward the two of them.

I sigh. It's hopeless to try and hide the way I feel from her. Besides, it would do me good to be able to talk to someone, especially now that they both know.

"I may get hurt, Jade. It's a risk I'm willing to take. I like the guy. I also know he's living in hell. How could he not be? That man will never get over the loss that some sick people caused him. He never will."

"You can't push him," she cuts me off before I spill those exact words out of my mouth.

"I'm not. Look," I say, then grab my Margarita from the bartender and turn back around to face her. "He and I have done as much talking as we have fucking. I know where he stands, he knows where I stand. I'm taking it one day at a time. Right now, what I'm going to do until we get down to helping him find the closure he needs, is take his mind off of it all. I may be a bitch for doing so, but that man over there, I take that back, both of those men over there deserve to have a good time. Now, I appreciate you caring about me, I really do. It makes me love the relationship you and I have more. If I need you, I promise to come to you. Right now though, I have a plan to get those two to have some fun. Are you with me?" I grab her hand away from the prowling eyes of the bartender. His gaze is glued to my chest, and I smile tightly as we turn and walk away, my toes stinging from the hot, white sand.

My voice is exceptionally low as we laugh over how to get those two in the water with us. This is me venturing into a territory I've never thought about before. The idea itself sends heat that doesn't come from the sun down my spine and spots in the center of my core. It's daring and erotic, and I'm ready to see what the two of them will do.

"You ready? I may not see you until tomorrow morning after this." Jade juts her hip out, places her empty hand on her hip, and drains her drink. I watch my brother out of the corner of my eye. His head follows her every move as she takes my empty cup from me, and I dip my body into the water and untie the string from around my neck, giving it a slight tug to loosen the string at my back.

She nods her head, walks up the beach, and tosses our cups into the trash, then starts to run toward the deserted part of the beach. I laugh my ass off as her top flings in the air right along with my brother jumping up like a brute force to be reckoned with. She really wants to be spanked like she said. I cringe, my mind not going there, because, well, it's my brother.

"Don't you dare stand up, or I swear I will bare your ass right here and turn it as red as half of these people's burnt skin." Kaleb is yelling at Jade, while Beau just crosses his arms over his chest. His stance is wide as my eyes roam down his body, landing on the ridge of his thick cock through his board shorts.

A wise teacher once told our class to never taunt an angry bear. I never listened to her boring speeches about animals in biology class. At the time, I was more interested in the natural science of the teenage boys in my class. This man standing at the edge of the water is definitely not a boy. No. He's all man. Thick, bulging arms, abs that have my mouth dry and desperately wanting to lick the salt from the ocean that's splattering on them the closer he gets to me with every step he takes.

"You wouldn't dare." I challenge him with a gleam in my eye that says I crave for him to slap my ass red.

"I would, and you damn well know it." He's within touching distance of me. I taunt him by leaning back into the water, submerging every part of me except my painfully swelled breasts. My nipples are hard in spite of the heat beating down from the sun.

"Fuck." He reaches for me before I get the chance to stand, a wave crashing over me, towing me under. He lifts my coughing body right out of the water, tosses me over his shoulders, and slaps my ass hard as he stomps through the throes of people who seem to find this funny.

"You asked for it. I told you to keep that on. No one, and I mean not even the old, wrinkled-up man over there with a bright-yellow speedo on is going to see this body. I'm going to fuck you until you listen." His words storm out of his mouth all the way to our room. They're still rumbling out even after he rips my bottoms off me, tosses me on the bed, and fucks me until I promise him I won't take it off again.

Fine. I promise…For now, anyway.

~~~~

"I've never been on a Jet Ski before. Are the two of you sure you can handle them?" Kaleb extends a hand to Jade, guiding her on the back of his like the instructor told him while my comment lures a teasing smile out of the guy who is rapidly stealing my breath away.

Last night flashes through my mind. Not the sex, although we did that enough times that I can say I shouldn't be turned on by his flashing smile or the way he scopes out my body. This skimpy black bikini I bought in the resort shop to replace the one he tore from my body actually looks better on me anyway. I'm so sore I can barely stand. Riding on the back of this isn't going to help the throb between my legs, that's for sure, but for him I'll endure the delicious pain as long as it keeps that magnificent smile growing.

"I handled you last night, quite thoroughly," he whispers, then reaches for my hand.

"You did? I thought it was the other way around." I grip the handles on the side and scoot my ass back far enough to allow him to hop on. My body fits against his perfectly.

When Kaleb starts his up, the roar of the engine drowns out Beau's next words that should make me blush. Instead, it zips a reminding pleasure so achingly painful through my body that if he doesn't start this damn thing, I'm changing my mind so we can go back and do it all over again.

"I'm not the one who lay spread eagled with her hands and feet tied to the bed and a towel stuffed in her mouth to stop her from screaming while I ate her sweet pussy for an hour straight before I untied her legs, whipped her around on all fours, and fucked her until she came twice, then marked her ass with my cum. That was you. Now hold on." I take in a sharp breath and let out an even harsher one when we speed off away from the dock. My arms slide from the handles to tightly wind around his waist.

"Oh my God," I scream loudly after we slow down enough to break over the waves and hit the dark-blue water.

The Jet Ski flies through the air over a wave caused by a boat, which scares the shit out me. We land hard on the water, and my ass smacks against the plastic. An explosive laugh rumbles from underneath the lifejacket Beau has on. The thing is plastered to his body so tightly I can't touch his skin. I may look like a cheesy, stupid fool with my own smile across my face, but I really don't care. He can't fake this. He really is having a good time. I glance over to Jade, who like me has a smile on her face as she stares with happiness at her best friend. We glance at each other briefly, both obviously thinking the same thing.

There are boats everywhere. Beau and Kaleb are soaring past them all. We head farther out and away from all the hustle of the touristy beaches and the potential agony that awaits us tomorrow when we all sit down for this meeting. All of it is left behind as I let the wind whip my hair out of my ponytail with my arms hugging him and my lungs inhaling the fresh, salty air.

I let go of him briefly to push my hair out of my face at the exact same time my brother slows down, signaling Beau to do the same.

"Jade and I are going to head this way." Kaleb hikes his thumb to the left of him.

"Go ahead. We'll go the other way," Beau hollers back. We wait until they've whipped around before he tells me why he decided to go in the opposite direction.

"I found a cove on the map when you were in the shower after breakfast. It's secluded. They need privacy too. You good with that?" He covers my hand with his. God, what am I doing? Even the smallest gesture, like him asking me if I'm okay with doing something he wants or the way he touches me has my heart leaping out of my chest.

"I'm good with it. Let's go," I say truthfully.

"Secluded is right." I look back behind us to see in the far distance and can barely make out the hustling atmosphere we left only a half hour or so ago when he slows down to a crawl the closer we get to the small, sandy beach. It's surrounded by a jungle of forest with a lot of foliage. It's primitive and definitely off of the power grid and hidden away from civilization.

"Did you bring me here to fuck me? If so, you know I'm willing." He laughs as he helps me off once we hit the sand. The water feels cool when I hop down into the ankle deep water.

"No, but if you're offering…" He lifts his hand to cup my face, pushing my hair out of his way, and gazes intensely into my eyes. I watch them magically turn from playful to heated to scorching dark.

"I saw this place in a brochure on the desk in our room. When Kaleb said he wanted to go the other way, it opened up the opportunity for me to bring you here. Alone. Here's your nude beach, Emmy. So strip." Oh fuck, oh shit. Is this really happening?

He moves quicker than I do, unsnapping his life jacket and tossing it on the ground. He tugs off his board shorts, leaving him naked with a very hard cock. I lick my lips and quickly mimic him as I strip myself bare. I'm throbbing with needy desire in spite of the aching between my legs and how badly I want to straddle him in the sand.

I bend over and pick up all of our stuff, then push him lightly backward until I have him close enough to a rock and out of view if anyone were to come upon us.

"Have a seat, Captain," I command him as I forcefully guide him back to where I want him. He sits down in the sand, and I toss our stuff to the side. I'm wet, he's hard, and all I want to do is keep making him smile, so I bend over and let him get a view of my pussy.

My nipples are hard, and I'm aching to feel him inside me. It's my mouth that gets him when I separate his stretched-out legs to crawl in between them.

"Fuck, Emmy." That's all he manages to say when I wrap my lips around his cock. I twirl my tongue across his tip, teasing him in a way that has him pulling the elastic entirely loose from my hair. He grips a handful of it and then begins to thrust his cock into my mouth, hitting my throat as he does.

"If you don't finger yourself and give me a fucking show, I will blister your goddamn ass." The way he speaks to me is like I'm one of his soldiers. His domineering voice is a turn-on that has me reaching for my clit with one hand and guiding my movements on his dick with the other.

I thought I was turned inside out, boiling over with lust for him last night, but today is even worse. He already has me topping the edge of a release. We may be playing dirty here, and I don't mean because I'm sucking his cock in the sand. I mean because of the situation we are in. His heart belongs to another, but I don't care anymore.

I'm past caring if I end up crying myself to sleep every night after he tells me he can't build a relationship with me. We're backwards, doing everything opposite of what a normal healthy relationship would start as. Fucking first, getting to know each other later.

"There are inches of that cock that you're not reaching. Take every single one. I want to see it all buried deep in that hot little mouth of yours." God, the man is a filthy talker. I'd be lying if I said his words along with his taste, his thrusts, and my fingers now sliding in and out of me aren't a turn-on.

I get up higher on my knees so I can take the rest of him into my mouth. My lips gladly slide down to where my hand is lightly stroking. His rhythm matches my pace. His pants mix with my moans. His hand pulls tighter on my hair as I bob, lick, and suck him like I own him.

When I feel my own release ready to crash into me like one of the waves in the ocean, I release my fingers and circle my clit eagerly.

"That's it. You need to come for me. It's right there, isn't it? You want to explode on your fingers. I'm almost there," he growls out. He's right. Even though no one can see us from where we are, this is the most daring thing I've done. None of the kinky stuff we did last night compares to feeling the sand on my knees, the hot sun beating on my ass while sucking a man I'm falling for with the water crashing into the rocks behind us.

When I feel my orgasm rip through me, I lay my tongue flat under the head of his dick and apply pressure to that sensitive spot. My hand moves, and when he comes in my mouth, I take it all.

CHAPTER SEVENTEEN

HARRIS

I'm standing next to Kaleb, waiting on this Samantha girl to come through these doors. We have a picture of what she looks like, and I can imagine she's going to be on guard the instant she sees the four of us. Kaleb and I both look like we're bouncers in a fucking club standing here with our arms crossed, so I try to stand at ease even with the stress pulling my muscles tighter by the second. The mere fact that Ty's siblings are standing here like vultures ready to dip down and attack isn't helping any of us either. Thank fuck we're standing far enough away that she won't notice us.

The second she walks through the side door to the front lobby where we were asked to wait, I know she's here. I watch every step she takes until Jade makes a move toward her after she greets the receptionist in her foreign language that's barely above a whisper. Emmy follows Jade, and I can tell the girl is startled when they introduce themselves. They both begin to talk quietly to her so as not make a scene, and before long, she agrees with a slight nod of her head before the three of them walk toward Kaleb and me, just like we hoped.

"Kaleb. Beau. This is Samantha. She's agreed to tell us what she knows for a few minutes, but she needs to get back to work shortly." I watch Samantha frantically look around behind her and can only imagine her issues if the wrong person sees her talking to us. She knows something. I can feel it. She's scared.

"What do you know about Ty Maverick?" Kaleb cuts to the chase. Her eyes can't hide the fact she knows him, but we already knew that.

"We used to date." Her voice is barely above a whisper. The way she talks low and soft tells me she doesn't want to talk to us here in the open. However, she also looks even more terrified now, and I begin to get even more apprehensive as she continues to look around us like she's worried about being watched.

"Can you tell us what you remember about the places he used to stay and the people he would run with?" She stops listening to Jade the second the door she just came through flies open.

In walks a little boy, four…maybe five years old, strutting his stuff and no doubt looking like a Maverick. *You have got to be shitting me?* My gut drops. What in the hell? There's no doubt that kid is…*Holy shit, Ty was a father.*

Samantha instantly begins to move around frantically, guiding the little boy out of the room and back through the door with the older woman he came in with. I pick up on her words she says in Spanish she throws at the woman. She's pissed off he was allowed out here after she specifically told her to keep him in the back room. My heart begins to thump as I think about what's happening here.

Kaleb and Emmy have both just found out their brother had a baby. The first child in the family, and neither of them knew anything about him. The shocked look on both of their faces saddens me, so I try to save this meeting with her before she runs or before Kaleb loses his temper and Emmy begins to cry with the unshed tears that are watering her eyes.

"Cute little guy you have there. Did Ty know he was a father?" She looks down and starts to fidget with her hands even more than she was before. Christ, this puts a whole new twist into this fucked-up mess. There's an innocent little boy involved here. No wonder she's a nervous wreck.

"He didn't care. He threw us away like we were trash." A tear falls down her cheek. I move to brush it from her face, but she ducks quickly as if I was about to hit her. This makes me feel like shit, and I realize I need to be careful with this one.

"I'm sorry. Can we just get this over with? What do you want from me? It's hard for me to do this. Ty was a terrible man, and frankly, I'm stunned here. My son looks so much like you and Ty." She points at Kaleb, and I now know where this is all going. She was terrified of Ty, and I'm sure it's justified.

"This is Kaleb. And this is Emmy. They are Ty's brother and sister." I point as Kaleb takes a step back, probably picking up on her fragility. Emmy moves closer, and I can tell her heart is feeling the small boy under the same roof with us right this very minute. She looks broken-hearted, and for a moment, my mind is not only on my own demands for this meeting, but on the two of them as well.

"I know who you are," she says. There is concern and fear radiating off of this woman like a beam full of pending doom. Shit is not right here.

"Can you help us? We need to see if you know anything that would help us with information about who killed my best friend." Her face freezes as if someone actually slapped her, which doesn't deter Jade's determination at all when she keeps moving forward. I stand back as well and let the women talk to her. The way she reacted to me only tells me she may respond better to them.

"I don't know anything." She's quick to respond and begins moving toward the door.

"Please. Someone killed my best friend. She was carrying a baby. Please give us just a little bit of your time to see if you can help. You're a mother, so I'm sure you understand how devastating this is for us." Jade's pleading grip on her arm seems to soften her face just enough that she nods to at least agree to another meeting.

"I really need to get to work now. Can you meet me tonight after work? I don't know if I can help, but I'll listen and see if I know anything. But we have to do it in privacy." She looks around like she's watching over her shoulder, so I do the same. When I don't see anyone of concern, I focus back on her.

"I leave here at three. Meet me at the bar in the back."
She walks away, and we all stand there in a fog of
astonishment. Jade moves to Kaleb and wraps her arms
around him. I watch Emmy's shoulders move inward as she
begins to process what just happened.

I have to hold her. I can't just let her feel like this and
stand by and watch. She doesn't open up to me when I wrap
my arms around her; she just stays frozen in a state of
disbelief even when I turn her so that I can hold her head
against my chest.

No one says a word. We don't make promises of
finding their nephew or scheme a plan to work Samantha
harder for information. That little boy changes everything, and
I hope his mother comes through with meeting us at three.
Something tells me she'll have a lead that will get us Mallory's
killer.

We all go to our rooms. Emmy still hasn't said a word. I
lie on the bed and watch her mind running in circles while I try
to think of something to make this better. Truth is, there isn't
much I can say. "You want to talk about it?" I ask.

She buries her head even further into the pillow before
she sits up and responds, taking the pillow with her, clinging it
to her chest for comfort. "It never even crossed my mind he'd
have a child. Now I'm wondering how many more there are.
How am I supposed to go home knowing someone related to
me lives in this hell? You can tell his mom is or was abused

by the way she reacted, which means he probably is too." I sit up to face her and try to reassure her when the truth is, I can't.

"I can only say we'll make sure he's protected before we leave. That's a promise I can make, but we have to see if she knows anything about Mallory." Her sad eyes immediately look into mine, and I see instant regret flash across her face.

"I'm sorry. I got so wrapped up in that little boy that I haven't focused on our real mission." She looks down at her hands that are clenching the pillow like it's her lifeline. I have to reach for her. I take the pillow out of her hands. If she needs something to hold on to, it's going to be me.

Drawing her into my arms, I let the first thing that comes to my mind blurt out. "I have enough focus for all of us. We'll get through this, Emmy. I won't stop until we find her killer and he's protected." I wipe a single tear from her eye before it runs down her beautiful face.

"I wonder what his name is," she whispers.

"We'll find out. I promise." She looks down again, and I decide to let her think about him and not try to distract her from it. He will forever be a part of her heart now. She's going to need time to adjust to the fact her brother had a child, a child she knew nothing about.

We only have a few hours until we meet Samantha again, so this can give me more time to prepare myself for questioning her.

We can't go in and interrogate her like all of the other people we have. She's going to have to be treated differently;

in fact, it's like we'll be tip-toeing around her, and that's
something at least three of us are not very good at.

"Kaleb looked shocked." Emmy's voice pulls me from
my thoughts. I just nod. He did. Hell, we all did. I'm sure he's
plotting some way to save the world for that little boy as we
speak, because in all honesty, it's what I'd do; and if I weren't
focused on finding Mallory's killer, I'd be doing it alongside
him.

My chest feels tight as I think about Mallory more and
more. The way Jade pleaded for Samantha to help and just
the mention of my baby pulled at every fucking heartstring I
have left.

Going into a meeting like this is something I'd generally
get pumped up for and let the adrenaline lead me through
getting the information. I'm trying to reel back that urge and go
into this like a civilian and just have a simple conversation with
her. Scaring her is only going to make her bottle up; I can tell
by what she has to loose. Even though we'd never hurt her
son, I don't know what kind of other threats are out there that
our visit here could bring her. It honestly wasn't a concern of
mine, until now that I know she has a Maverick in her life.

"We'll find her killer. I won't leave your side until we do."
I can feel Emmy's eyes on me even through all of my scattered
thoughts. I'm used to a game plan and feel like we're going in
blind on this mission.

"Thank you." What else can I say? We're officially in
this together now more than ever, and I just hope we can get

what we need from Samantha and get home before we try to do anything with the boy. It would make me feel better to have the girls on home soil before anything happens that may require us to possibly return back here. I hate this damn country, but there are answers here. I know it. Answers I need so I can get my revenge. I try to lock the memories I have of Mallory and me in a special place that will never die. I need a spot where love will always remain and for her to know I loved her enough to make sure justice was done in my own way.

"She seemed scared. Maybe I can offer her and her son a home in The States. I'm sure Kaleb can get them a legal citizenship because of Ty's terrorist situation with the government." The sound of Emmy's loving voice brings me to stare at the incredible woman before me. What she's saying is a possibility, but whenever you involve government officials, there's a chance it won't work out how we hope.

"Kaleb may already have that in motion." If I know him at all, he's already working on it. He has strings he can pull, and there's no doubt in my mind he'll use them for family. Family is the one thing he holds very close to his heart. His mother and sister are proof of that, and Ty would've been if he hadn't turned into an international criminal.

"Maybe we should go to their room and start talking about this. We need to all be on the same page when we meet her. I want to see that boy again. I need to know more about him before we leave here." I agree. I do need her to know one thing before we head out first though.

"I want you to know that I can't imagine how you're feeling right now, but I'm here for you if you need to talk more. And I swear to you, Emmy, no matter what we find out, I'll do everything to make sure that little boy is protected." Her response seems pained in the way she smiles tightly but doesn't respond.

I reach for her hand and guide her up before we both walk toward the door. The minute the door shuts behind us, the smell of the salty air that should fill my senses with the mere fact we're in paradise does the opposite. It fills me with dread that we're about to fall into a web of deceit much worse than finding out about a little boy no one knew existed.

"Hey." Jade answers the door with her phone to her ear. The minute Emmy sees Kaleb standing on the deck, she lets go of my hand. She's in his arms right away, letting the floodgates from their hell open while she cries.

"Hang on a minute, Steele." Jade pulls the phone away from her ear, grabs a little silver clutch, and gestures for me to follow her out the door.

"Find out everything you can about him. There has to be a birth certificate. I also want to know how we can get him across the border if she agrees come with us." She pauses, and all I can hear is Steele firing off a shit ton of questions at her. "I know all that shit. Just do it." Pulling the phone away from her ear, she tucks it in her little bag, dragging my ass out of the room behind her and to the nearest bar.

"What the hell was that all about?" I demand.

"Kaleb is a mess. I'm doing what he asked me to while he gets his shit together. How's Emmy?" She rattles off without telling me what she's doing. I have a feeling I know, but I'd feel better having that shit confirmed.

"Needing her brother," I say truthfully. They need to sort this out together. It's a hard blow to both of them. I can't even think about how their mom is going to take it. No doubt she'll fall completely apart.

"I'll take a Corona. Hold the lime, please," she tells the bartender when she approaches.

"What would you like?" the perky little dark-haired woman whose gaze runs up and down my body seductively asks.

"Water is good." I ignore her look all together. Jade goes to speak, but I silence her with a lift of my hand until the bartender delivers her beer and my water, never taking her eyes off of me. I hate women who are blatantly obvious when they look at you like they want to fuck your brains out without caring if you're standing next to another woman or not. For all this chick knows, Jade and I could be together. The urge to tell her to have some respect sits on the edge of my tongue, but I let it slide, because there are more important things to discuss than telling her I have no interest in her at all.

"Kaleb wants to know everything he can about that little boy before we meet her. He lost it when he tried explaining to Steele. God, Harris, this is bad. Something isn't right here. That woman is scared out of her mind to talk to us. Did you see the look on her face when she saw Kaleb? It was like she saw a ghost." I can't miss the fright expelling from Jade or the way she guzzles half of her beer in one swallow. She's as worried as I am.

"They look a hell of a lot alike. Can't say I blame her for freaking the fuck out. She handled herself well, but there's more. I don't give two fucks what it is she's hiding from. I'm not leaving that damn meeting until she tells us everything."

"We'll get to the bottom of it. Now, I need to know how you're doing. And I mean really doing. No bullshit, no saying what you think I need to hear." Well, shit. I could use something heavier than a glass of water to oust all the emotions that are pushing and pulling me in every direction. Except I need my head clear for this meeting. What she tells us will determine whether I grab a bottle of tequila and drown my reactions in it or not.

"I'm hanging in there, if that's what you mean?" It's a vague answer.

"Thanks for pointing out the obvious. I think you know what I mean." She places her hand on my arm in a friendly gesture.

"It's killing me. Is that what you need to hear again?" I spit out. "I feel guilty for sharing a bed with someone else.

And shame for not pulling my head out of my ass sooner to find out who killed her. I'm disgusted with myself, because my heart is holding on to something that will never be. So the truth is, fuck no. I'm not okay. I've got a woman who I can't promise a thing to who I know wants more than I can give her. She's a good woman, and the thing is, I don't even know if once we get the answers we need, I'll be able to give her what she deserves."

CHAPTER EIGHTEEN

EMMY

All I see is the look on that little boy's face through my hazy fog of tears. My God, his eyes are the same shape as ours, deeply set and prominent to the extent they dominate his tiny facial features. The only thing separating him and the way Ty looked is the color of his skin and hair. He has his mother's complexion and dark hair, although while I stand here soaking my brother's shirt with tears, clinging on to him because I can't let him go, I remember everything about her too. She's beautiful in a way I can't explain. Her exotic look of possibly half Spanish and half American nearly left me breathless to know that Ty was involved with someone so beautiful.

"I don't understand any of this, Kaleb. How could he do this? He not only threw us away like we meant nothing to him, he threw away his own child. What kind of person does that kind of stuff? I...oh God. How are we going to tell Mom? She's still hurting. This is going to break her." I sob into his chest more. I let go for so many reasons.

I cry for the boy, my brother, her, me, all of us. I let it out until I don't think I can cry anymore, but then I do. I cry again, until finally I'm pulled away from Kaleb, looking into his glassy eyes as well.

"Sis. We have to stop. No more of this. I know it feels like there's no ending in sight here when it comes to the shit he's done. The one good thing he did in his life was help create that little boy, then walk away from him. Ty was a piece of shit, but he was our brother, and now, even though we lost him a long time ago, we can do right by his son. We have to show that boy he has another family. It's a shocker to both of us, but we need to get a grip and deal with what we came down here to do. Then we focus on Mom." He stops talking only to walk a few steps away from me and start again.

"I know what we have to do. We have to center our attention on that nephew of ours. His piece of shit dad may not have wanted anything to do with him, but that kid is part of us, Emmy. We deserve to know him as much as he deserves us. Now, go get cleaned up in your room. Once we talk to her, I'm sure she'll understand we aren't like him." I shudder when I tear my gaze from his. His words of how selfish and what a deadbeat of a man our brother was only make me angrier at Ty for all of this. What Kaleb is saying is true, and now we need to make sure this all ends right here and now.

"Okay. Are you sure you'll be alright? I mean," I gesture around their suite when I realize both Jade and Beau are gone. I'm assuming they gave us the space we needed to come to terms with this life-changing little boy who has stunned our systems in an indescribable way. "They took off," I finish.

"I'm going to hop in the shower to clear my head before I go find them. Jade was finishing up a phone call for me when you busted in here. I'm sure they went to the bar by the pool or some shit. I'm good. You?" He dips his head down to my level.

"I will be. Are you going to ask her to let us see him?" I know I acted crazy when I expressed to Beau I wanted to bring him back to The States with us. If I lived here and had a son, there would be no way in hell I would allow my young child to visit strangers in a foreign country, no matter if I were with him or not. It's going to be hard enough for her to explain to him who we are.

"She's hiding something," I blurt out.

"She is. Something tells me we aren't going to like it either. I have a feeling whatever it is, she's still living it. That woman is being abused and threatened, and I have every reason to believe she's living in a defenseless corner. I can imagine her backed up against the wall, because whoever the hell is causing her to be scared is terrorizing her with the only weakness she has." His words are bitter-tasting as I inhale them all, letting them sink to the depths of my soul.

"The boy. She's being harassed to keep her mouth shut, or they will do something to him." I gasp as those words fall out of my mouth. This is bad. Worse than I can imagine.

"I'm sure. But don't you worry that pretty little head of yours, little sister. We'll get to the bottom of all of this. Now, go. I got some shit to do. Ring me when you're ready. We'll find those two and derive a plan before we meet with Samantha. I'll get a pile of answers to questions she has no idea are coming."

"You need to be careful with her, Kaleb. No blowing up at her. No raising your voice. She's fragile." I know my brother; he may have a big heart, but when it comes to getting answers, he won't let a damn thing get in his way.

"Maybe you should talk to her then. I mean, isn't psychoanalyzing a person right up your alley?" He raises a brow as well as his voice at me.

"No. I'm not going to school to be a shrink. Although maybe I should so I can pull your head out of your ass."

"Seriously. I think it's a great idea if she talks with you, Emmy. We all know she's hiding something. Whatever it is, she's scared out of her mind over it. I have a feeling that Ty was smack in the middle of her fears," Jade walks in and pipes in calmly with her words, yet restlessly with her meaning.

"I'll stay quiet until she says something I don't like. You good with this, Stone?" Beau has been quiet for most of the afternoon. I'm not sure what's going through his head.

The closer we got to this meeting, the more restless he became, which is completely understandable. He even went as far as to pack his bags already. For what, I'm not sure. It's as if he's switched off the light in his head and went completely dark on me. I've left him alone with his thoughts, knowing this has to be hard for him. He's possibly one step closer to finding out answers he needs to be able to find closure, which I pray he finds no matter the outcome of this meeting.

"I'm good with it. Don't any of you think for one minute that if she knows a thing about what happened to Mallory, how we handle it isn't up to anyone of you. This is my damn call." I keep my mouth purposefully shut, even though I desperately want to tell both of these overbearing assholes to go back to the rooms or shut the fuck up.

I don't say any of that though, because we all turn at the same time to the click of high heels across the pool deck. She appears to be a little calmer than this morning, except her eyes are still scanning the area like a madwoman. She's nervous, slightly investigating her surroundings, almost like she's being watched or scared she might be.

The closer she gets to us, the more nervous I am. *You can do this, Emmy.* I make an effort to give myself the mental courage to do so.

"Hello," she bites out nervously. "Would you care if we go to one of your rooms and talk? There are too many people out here. You never know who might be listening in." She scans the area one more time before looking back at the four of us.

"Sure, wherever you're more comfortable," I answer politely.

"Well, I'd truly be more comfortable if you'd all leave and never come back," she snaps.

"Never going to happen, sweetheart. Whether you give us answers to why we're here or not, especially now that we know about the boy." I toss Kaleb one hell of a dirty look. I should've known he wouldn't keep his mouth shut. She says nothing as we follow her through the same area we came in, weaving through the beautiful scenery that doesn't seem beautiful anymore, not with the heaviness weighing on our hearts.

Once we reach our room, I slide in the keycard, push the door open, then silently close it once we're all inside.

"Let me tell you one thing before you start shooting at me with your questions. My son's name is not boy. It's Gabriel. I hate the word boy. So please, don't address him like that again." I can see she is extremely upset about this, not only by the way she narrows her eyes at Kaleb, but by how thick her Spanish accent became. This morning, there was only a hint of it.

"Yes, Gabriel Capo Lewis. He's named after both of your parents. Gabriel after your father, who is American. His middle name is your mother's maiden name. She is from here. Lewis must be a surname." Jade shocks us all as she begins to spit out all of that information. I try to soften the conversation and not come at her like these barbarians are.

"I love that name. You must care very much for your parents to name your son after them." I take a seat and pat the spot next to me for her. "Gabriel would be my nephew. It makes me sad I've missed so much of his life. I'm not like my brother. This guy here isn't either. We tried so hard to make him see what he was doing was wrong; we just couldn't get through to him. He's dead now, and we feel so guilty for not knowing he had a son."

Out of my peripheral I watch the other three sit. When there's no response from Kaleb, I continue. "He can't hurt you ever again, and if we had known, we would've made sure you were both safe. Do you think you might be able to help us with our friend's murder? We want to end the torture and find some closure." I work to pull the questions as to why we need her help in the first place.

"Let me start by saying I'm sorry about your friend. I truly don't know anything about anyone dying, but I...I may know someone who does."

"Who?" Beau bellows out, causing us both to jump.

"Oh God, where do I start?" Samantha whispers, her eyes on the verge of shedding tears.

"The beginning." Beau leans forward in his chair. His eyes are blazing toward us. I try to block her from seeing how mean he looks.

She blows out a long breath and swipes at her eyes. "Several years ago, I met Ty in a bar. I was nineteen years old, working my way up the ladder for my parents, learning everything I could. Well, anyway. I fell for him. I thought he fell for me too. For almost an entire year, he never missed a weekend with me. I decided to surprise him at home on his birthday with the news I had found out that day. I had no idea how he was going to take it. I just knew I had to tell him." She pauses with a light chuckle.

"He was fucking another woman while she cried and screamed horribly. I stood there not knowing what to do, until finally, I backed up to leave. I managed to get home without him knowing it. For weeks, I hid at another one of my dad's resorts. I threw my phone away, begged my parents to let me work there. I did it all to stay away from him. I was scared for my baby. That's the news I wanted to tell him. I had no idea at the time what I walked in on, but I knew it wasn't good. I wanted nothing more to do with him." She pauses to catch her breath. Not one of us wavers to interrupt her.

"He found me. I was barely showing when I told him. It didn't stop him from beating me. He broke my leg, my arm, and my collarbone. I screamed, cried, and begged him I wouldn't tell a soul what I saw if he left me alone. He left me alone alright, with a promise that if I ever told a soul, he would take my baby. I haven't told anyone until now."

I don't even realize I have tears running down my face until the wetness hits my bare legs. I look to Jade, who's bawling right with me. Kaleb's expression has barely changed; he's either assessing her for the truth, or he's waiting for more.

And Beau. I know he's waiting. He's been waiting for a clue since the second she started talking.

"Why are you talking about it today?"

"Because he's dead and can't hurt me anymore."

"Can you tell us who you think killed Mallory?" Beau stands, his tall frame towering over the both of us.

"I believe it was Amato Esteban. He was the man your brother was working for. He's one of Mexico's biggest drug lords." I study her features, the way she wrings her hands as she talks and keeps glancing to the floor as she continually refuses to look Kaleb in the eye.

"There's more, isn't there? What are you not telling us?" I stand next to Beau. My voice is louder than I want it to be, but this has gone on long enough.

"It's not that easy." She stands face-to-face with me.

"Bullshit. Are you being threatened again? Is that what it is? This Amato is threatening my nephew, isn't he? He has you doing stuff for him, am I right?" I'm shaking now. I have no idea what she has gone or is going through, but my God, maybe she likes being yelled at or berated. I don't know. I can hear Kaleb texting someone and can only assume he's sending word to one of the guys to dig up as much information on this guy as he can.

"I can't tell you anything. You don't know these men. They will take him from me, and he will be turned into one of them."

"That's enough! We will do everything to protect you. You don't have to worry about that anymore. You're still not giving us the answer we need. Why would he kill her?" This time it's my brother who hollers.

Her eyes close, her lips tremble.

"HOW. DO. YOU. KNOW?" Kaleb yells.

"He told me, alright!" she cries out. "He said you sealed your own fate when you came here. He's going to kill you all."

"Really? Well, where is he, if he knows we're here? Call him up, tell him to get his fucking ass here." Beau is livid, and I see a new side of him surfacing the more she talks.

"I can't."

"And why is that?" Beau asks.

"I'm supposed to use Gabriel to get you to go to him."

CHAPTER NINETEEN

HARRIS

What in the fuck. This is turning into a disaster. All I want to do is find Mallory's killer and make sure this little boy is safe, and now I'm paranoid about keeping the girls safe. Every single hair on my body is standing at attention. I want to lose my shit, but I can't. I have to remain calm and collected to get us through this.

"What do you mean, he's using Gabriel?" She jumps at the sound of my voice. I don't blame her. I'm angry, and it's hard to hide that.

"I'm supposed to make you come to me so he can get to you all. He wants blood for what you did." All the possibilities of what could happen flash through my mind and terrify me entirely. He could literally take everything that means anything to me if he gets to these girls. Jade is my best friend, and I can't stand the thought of her getting hurt. Emmy has quickly made her way into my life, and another loss would ruin me for good.

"We have to beat him at his own game then. We'll go in loaded and ready to counter anything he tries. We'll make sure you're safe before we leave, even if that means taking you back to The States, where I can guarantee your son's safety." Kaleb keeps talking, and I watch her take his words in.

"I have to make sure Gabriel is safe."

"You have my fucking word. We just need you to help us get this guy so we can all get the fuck out of here." Kaleb looks at me with just as much hysteria as I feel. If I thought I had a lot to lose in this, he beats me hands down. Losing his sister or his woman would be the end of Kaleb, plus now he has a nephew.

I step closer to him, so he's the only one who can hear me. "We'll get through this. We don't have any other fucking choice, man. Let's regroup and come up with a plan of attack. And don't even think about taking the girls in on this one. I'm going in guns fuckin' blazing, and I don't want anything in my way. We can lock them in our suites and get them once we're done."

"We have to move them. I don't trust one fucking thing the woman says. She may be setting a trap in both directions. If he knows we're here, we're fucked. Like goddamn sitting ducks waiting for hell to rain on us again. Did I fucking say I hate Mexico? Because I do fucking hate this place." Kaleb is just as pissed as I am, and I know what he's saying is true. We have to take every step with precaution and make sure we do this right. I don't want anyone hurt in this.

"Where's your son? You're going to need him with you. We'll move you until we get back so we know you're safe." I'll move her with the girls, and taking the boy will only verify they'll all be safe. She's not going to want to draw the evil toward her kid.

"I can't involve him."

"You already did. We have to know he's safe before we go in and take care of shit. You don't want him on the other side of what we're about to do." She finally looks at me, and I can see the fear in her eyes. She's fucking terrified, and she should be.

"He has him." Fuck. How in the fuck am I going to go in there and shoot up shit when I know a kid is in there? A Maverick kid at that. "Goddamit. How am I supposed to believe you? You come in here telling us everything we want to hear and acting like you're protecting us. How do I know this isn't part of your fucking plan?"

"I guess you'll have to trust me." Jade stands as soon as Samantha responds, and I know what's about to go down now.

"I don't have to do a fucking thing. You see, we're here to get some information. You've already told us the name of who you think is the killer. Why do we need to do anything else? We can get the fuck out of here and leave you to deal with your own mess." Jade's icy glare is forcing Samantha back against the wall.

"Because I can take you to him. I can help you end all of this, and if you don't, you'll always be looking over your shoulder waiting for the next attack on your perfect little team." Samantha's response makes Jade snap. She has her arm into her throat the second she finishes the sentence.

"I'll fucking end this all for you right now. If you're sending us into some fucked-up trap, just know that I'll be the one torturing you on the opposite side. You'll wish to whatever God you believe in that you had never met me. You see, I don't give a fuck about Ty's kid. He was always a piece of shit to me. These other three I'm with have ties to this mission. I'm just here to make sure shit gets done. I won't leave any fucking loose ends, and that means you, if that's what it takes." Samantha begins to tremble even more. Emmy stands and places her hand on Jade's shoulder, only pissing Jade off even further.

"Get the fuck off of me. I'm not doing this Mexico shit again. She stays with me. If anything goes wrong, I'll personally be her hell." I can see the same crazy in Jade's eyes I saw when Fire was kidnapped. She's scared, and she's making sure she has leverage in this mission. I get what she's doing. It's a scare tactic. It also allows Samantha to think Emmy is a friend to her because she stood up to Jade. *Fucking brilliant, girls.*

It's all a mind game at this point. We have to make her not turn on us. If she does, we'll have to decide how to handle it from there.

"Let's move. Get everything from the suites that's important. The rest we hand off to someone on the beach."

"He already knows where we are. He's expecting me to bring you to him. If we do anything different, he kills Gabriel." The silence in the room is deafening. We all stand there knowing what we have to do, yet no one wants to acknowledge it.

"We have to go." Emmy is the first to speak up. "We have to get revenge for Mallory, and I have to save my nephew. Even if it means I go alone."

"You're out of your fucking mind. I'm not taking you girls in there. No fucking way." Kaleb slams his hand hard on the bar, sending a loud rumble through the room.

"Kaleb. I'm not doing this bullshit with you again. I'm a fucking soldier when we're out on these missions. We go in as if I am any of your guys, and you shut the fuck up about it. It's not like you have any other choice or some place to hide us." Jade meets Kaleb face-to-face.

"Do you really think I have you here without a fucking backup plan?" He moves closer to me, so that I'm the only other person in the room who can hear what he says to Jade. "I need you to go in a separate vehicle that will arrive when ours does. I have a man on standby just outside the resort. You go with him and do exactly what he says."

"Kaleb. I won't leave you again. Fuck off."

"Jade. I won't go into this trap with you. I need you to keep my sister safe and promise me you'll find my nephew if something happens to me."

"No. I'm not doing this. You two aren't going in on this alone. I've proven myself over and over again." Jade isn't calming down at all as she starts to talk even louder.

"Shhhh. And that's why I'm giving you Emmy to take care of. I know she's safe with you." He pulls her closer. I have to take a step back. This is a lover's quarrel, and I can see both sides of it, but honestly, I'm tired of waiting to move.

"Kaleb. I can't do this again. I won't. You either take me with you, or you know what I have to do." She silences him as he stares into her eyes. I know she means business, and I hope he knows as well.

"We need to move before this guy gets a clue about what we're doing. We have to act fast, and you both know it. So decide who's going with me and who's not before I leave by my motherfucking self." I have zero fucks to give at this point. I know this is important to the both of them, but I refuse to let time pass and let this window of opportunity to find the fucker go by while we're still talking.

"Let's go. I'm ready." Jade turns to me, responding quickly, and I know I need to start moving now if I'm going to get these two to come together. Kaleb is infuriated. I get it, but we have a mission to finish.

"What are we doing with Emmy? She's not trained for this shit." I stop dead in my tracks. I fucking don't know what to do with her. I just know I have to move now. My focus is blinding me of anything else besides going to find Mallory's killer. Right. The fuck. Now.

"What if I take two of you to him and then we can turn the tables on him once we have my son? Two of you can stay back and follow us in. He'll believe I could only get a few of you to come with me."

"I'm going in," Kaleb speaks up instantly.

Jade follows before I have a chance to even speak up. "We'll go together. You told him we were couples, right?"

"Fuck off, Ice. I'm not letting you walk into a trap like this and use you for bait." I have to try to talk some logic into this girl. She wants to save the fucking day, but I'll be damned if I'm going to sit back and twiddle my thumbs while she's going in scapegoat for me. I'm the one with the bone to pick, and I need to do this.

"We need to send the right people in and have the right people as backup. You know this, Harris. You and Emmy can come in behind us and surprise everyone." She's trying her hardest to make it seem logical, but she's being ridiculous.

"No. Emmy and I need to go in. They'll capture us instantly, and then you and Kaleb can come in and bust shit up. We'll just hang tight until you get there." She laughs at my response.

"Hang tight? What if they start to torture you or move you before we can fucking get there?" Jade is the only one talking back to me. I know Kaleb knows this is the best move, because I can see him looking at Emmy with fear across his face.

"Ice. Stop. They're going in, and we will take it over within minutes of them crossing the threshold. We will let the element of surprise work for us." Kaleb moves to take Jade into his arms. I can feel Jade's cold stare on my back as she takes in what's about to happen.

"She's not trained for this shit." She attempts one last time to convince Kaleb to change his mind.

"She won't need to be to go in as a decoy, but you know we need you coming in to handle shit like you do so well." He moves in closer and continues to talk as I walk over to Emmy to see where her head is.

"You in for this?" Before I can finish everything I want to say, she interrupts me.

"Yes. I can do this. I have to, because we need to know what happened, and if there's a chance I can save Gabriel, I have to try." She's terrified, and honestly, I don't blame her. We're literally going in blind and won't have any weapons on us. The first thing he'll do is check us. We need to try and buy as much time as we can to distract them.

"Samantha. What does he know about us?" I try to come up with the best story for all of us. We have to get our shit together on this and make sure we don't fuck anything up. I can't have anything going wrong in this.

"He knows you're here to see me and that you've asked about Ty. He plans to make you talk about Al-Quaren's location, because he's apparently the source of all the money in their business." So he needs information. I can use this to our advantage, but that means he only needs one of us, so taking Emmy is a danger.

"I'm going solo. You will tell him the others left. I don't fucking care, but I'm going in solo." I push Samantha back against the wall. Her eyes meet mine as she nods her head up and down at me without saying a word.

"I'll be right on your ass, so just go in and get me the Intel I need to do this shit." Maverick hands me a tiny device that attaches to my hair and then starts to put his own earpiece in. Jade does the same as Emmy stares at the one he just handed her.

"If anything starts to go down, you get your asses in there and save the kid." I glare at Maverick to make sure he knows I mean business. He gestures with a quick tilt to the head that he understands me. I can't help but wonder if this is where it all ends. I've never been more unprepared for a mission in my life. I've also never been this personally tied to it.

They say it's never good to mix personal issues in this field of work, but how can I not when I have revenge to seek? This is what I was born to do, and this may as well be what I die doing. Whatever the outcome of this is, I just hope we can save the kid.

I gather Maverick and Jade in the corner, and Emmy follows. I decide to tell them a few things before we go in. "Alright, new mission. This is now a rescue mission to save the kid. We do what it takes to get him and his mother to safety. If it means you leave me behind, then you fucking do it." Jade instantly starts to disagree, but I hold my finger to her mouth. "Shhhh. I'm not arguing on this. I'm going in. You follow my ass in there, and I expect to hear one hell of an entrance from all of you within a few minutes of me arriving."

This may be the most dangerous thing I've done. I'm not covered in a way I was on our missions in the Army. This time, it's a one-man team going in with a small crew following closely. I have to say the odds aren't in my favor, but nonetheless, I have to do this.

I take one last look at Emmy and the sadness in her eyes. She knows how dangerous all of this is. She's not an idiot. I can tell by the way she's looking at me that she's worried out of her mind about how this is going to turn out. Fuck. If I could turn back time, I never would've suggested she come here. Hell, I would've come by myself and kept the entire team safe from the shit that's about to go down here.

"I have ears on you, Stone. Pierce, show me what you know about this guy. Tell me what we're going in on." Stone. There it is. My call name on missions. Maverick has switched to mission talk, and I'm so fucking thankful it's time. It's time to see that Fire and Ice in action again. "Emmy will be called Midnight. If there's any correspondence on air, make sure you use call names."

I watch as very little information comes through on Maverick's phone about this guy. He's fucking good. Of course, he is. One of Mexico's best drug lords isn't going to be a sloppy one. I know with more time we would've been able to find something out, but I already know what I need to.

He's a piece of shit who deserves to die. Even if he isn't the one who killed Mallory and my child, he's holding a little boy as bribery right now, and that shit just doesn't sit well with me.

I can't look at Emmy anymore. She's not where my head needs to be. Her fear and confusion will only stir up chaos as I go into this. "Let's fucking go. Samantha, take me to this motherfucker."

I feel Emmy's hand slide under my arm just as I order the girl to take me. Her hands wrap around my waist from behind, and I stop breathing as she squeezes me tight. I don't return the affection; I just look forward. This is something I can't give her when I'm not even sure if I'll come out of this alive.

"Beau, please be safe." Her soft whisper against my back sends a chill over my body as she slowly pulls away. She's lifted her body from mine before I move, so it's only her hand I can reach when I finally pull out of my trance.

"Emmy. I hate that I brought you here. I wish like hell I could go back and just slip away from the compound and not be in this predicament today. You don't deserve this." Even though tears are filling her eyes, I turn and walk away. Samantha leads me from the suite, and I let Fire handle what I'm walking away from.

I have to stay focused. This is the moment I've been dreaming of for months. I just need one second with this fucker, and all of the things I've imagined will finally be at my fingertips.

I'm about to kill a motherfucker.

CHAPTER TWENTY

EMMY

I'm scared out of my mind. Beau is walking away from us, and I can't shake this feeling that things will never be the same after this.

We start to move with fast feet until we get to an old van just outside of the resort.

"It's about fucking time. I was wondering if you were on a permanent vacation out here." Kaleb and Jade slide in, and I follow. Kaleb says a few things to the man driving that I don't hear because I can't seem to slow down the screaming in my mind about what's about to happen. There are two guys. One is driving, and the other is in the front passenger seat. I can tell Kaleb knows them, and that makes me feel better. We have a few more going in with us, which can only help our odds.

"Emmy, take this and stay on our ass. We'll be moving fast. Remember everything I taught you." My brother is different. He's hard and cold as he hands me two pistols and talks to me in a rush. Jade looks so serious, and honestly, the feeling in the air is icy. There's no room for mistakes or any nonsense.

This is what I imagined it would be like on one of their missions. Everyone is focused and ready to kill. The van is moving at an insane rate of speed down the road as I work to shift my heart from racing rapidly to zoning in on the anger that this Mexican guy has caused my family. If he was whom Ty worked for, then I have so much more to hate this man for than what we're here to deal with today.

I let my mind fall to some of the memories of how it felt every time we heard from Ty and the fucked-up mess he was in. I still can't believe that even in death he's tearing this family apart. His efforts to be a terrible man never did stop shocking me.

Swallowing hard, I decide to make it my personal mission to let this all end here. Ty won't be able to do this to us anymore. We will get through this, and we'll get to know his son even though he decided to toss him away. In all actuality, he did the little guy a favor. He needs to be far away from this lifestyle, and that's why I'm going in.

I take the guns Kaleb gave me and flip the clip to see a full load on both. This is a gun I'm very used to using, and it does make me feel better knowing I could load this in my sleep. Jade hands me two extra clips, which I tuck into my bra. I don't have anything else on me, so I guess this will have to do.

I'm trying to compose myself and at the same time hanging on as this guy's driving speeds us through the streets. He seems to know where he's going, and I do my best to take in every turn he takes as well as our surroundings as we go. I think I've got this and this is all something I can handle until the reception in my ear comes on.

"He's almost there. All ears on until this is over."
Maverick's voice catches as he hears Beau start talking.

"Why are you still in Mexico when you knew your son
was still in danger?" Beau is obviously still talking to
Samantha, and I love that he's worried about Gabriel even with
all the heartache he's trying to avenge in this.

"Because they'd just find me. If I don't run, maybe they
won't notice me." She sounds defeated even though she's
going in with a few of the most elite members in the United
States, but how is she to know how qualified these three are?
I may not be as experienced as they are, but I have the heart
to get through this and do anything it takes to save that little
guy. He looks so much like my brother was when he was
younger, and if I'm being honest, I would like another chance
at being there for him. This time, I'll make sure he's never put
in the path to become a monster like his father was.

"This is where we'll park. We'll go in all doors as soon
as you give the go, Fire." I look around and continue to listen
to Beau talk. He seems calm, and that does so much to calm
the insanity in my head.

"I'm going to get your son from this asshole and then
I'm going to help you get away from here. Can you promise
me that you'll come to The States with us so we can help
you?" I listen to my earpiece closely, trying to hear what she
says, but I never hear her say anything. The sound of car
doors opening and closing is what comes through before the
wind begins to whistle through the speaker.

"Fuck. He better not be messing with that fucking piece. I'll kick his ass." Jade, well I guess it's Ice out here, yells out as she holds her hand over her ear trying to hear just like I am. It takes a few seconds before we hear him again.

The angry sound of foreign men pours into my ear, and I quickly go from calm to terrified. I have no idea what they're saying, but I can hear at least three different, distinct voices.

A grumble from Beau comes through, and Kaleb quickly speaks up. "We have three that he can see." They must have a secret code of grunts and grumbles that gives information without giving anything away.

It's only a few seconds before I hear the horrible sound of Beau groan after a series of punches. The disgusting sound of filth fills my ears as I hear him being yelled at, while all along all we do is sit here and wait.

"Why aren't we moving?" Kaleb holds his hand up for me to stop talking, so I do. It takes everything inside me to be patient and not open this door and run to him. My only problem is, I have no idea where I'm going, and we all know I have no idea what to do once I get there.

"They're questioning him about the last mission we were on. We have to give him a chance to get some information from them before we blow those fuckers up." Jade leans in to explain the situation a little better to me. I'm glad someone can understand the language being spewed at him.

The next thing I hear is Beau talking to them in their native tongue. I can't fucking understand a word he's saying, and if I thought I was lost and scared before, this moment right here brings a whole new meaning to that. I look to Jade for answers, and she leans back again to tell me more.

"He's fishing to see if they knew Ty, which we already knew they did. Don't worry, we're experienced in this shit. He knows what he's doing." Even though she's trying to calm me, she doesn't. The sound of their voices tells me they are angry at him, and I know when someone has a disgust for a person like I can hear, then they are past the point of being rational, not that these men can be sane doing what they do.

I hate that I never learned this language. Not that I ever want to be in this situation again, but I think that's going to be on my list of things to do in the very near future...if I survive this day.

CHAPTER TWENTY-ONE

HARRIS

I have to get more information from these guys before Fire and Ice come in and fuck everything up. I work hard to stay in the mindset to play these games with this rotten-toothed motherfucker.

After taking about ten kicks to the stomach and a few elbows to the face, I can barely see and my breathing is a struggle to say the least. They have me tied to a chair, but I'm working on the knot every chance I get. I've counted three visible enemies, and I haven't seen Gabriel yet. Samantha finally asks for him. They smack her to the ground before she can get the entire sentence out.

I focus on her crying to dig deeper so I can power through whatever they throw at me.

The back door opens, and in walk two more men, one of them in a white suit strutting like he owns the place. I'm going to guess that is my guy. If he's not, he one of the guys I plan to end here today.

"Mr. Beau Harris. How are you, my little friend?" His English is shitty and hard to make out, but I can and do.

"I'm not your fucking friend." I spit at his feet to match his squared-up lips of disgust as he looks at me.

"You come here and spit at my feet. You make it much easier to take care of business. Maybe I fuck your black-haired angel before I kill her." My stomach churns with his words, and the anger I felt before only flows hotter now. I'm going to kill this motherfucker, and if he's lucky, I won't skin him alive first.

"I don't have a black-haired angel."

"Don't play games with me. I've been watching you, just like I watched you with your last piece of ass." He moves in closer, allowing his skank-ass breath to brush over my nose as he continues to talk. The only reason I'm not slamming my head into his face is because I want to hear him say it. I want to hear him say he killed her, so I can fucking mutilate his ass.

I look up to him and dare him to continue. Of course, he does. "It was such a beautiful day. You need to learn to watch the area around you. If you hadn't been looking at her like that, you would've seen me coming." He stands quickly, knowing my head is coming for his face. His words send my gut into a whirlwind of hatred as I watch him move a few steps around the room before he passes back by. *Fire, get your ass in here and let me kill this piece of garbage.*

It's as if he could hear me. Within a few seconds, the doors are all busting open and fog fills the room while shots are flying everywhere. I drop to my side and begin to work my wrists free. Samantha crawls to me, and it's only a short time before I can hear Jade yelling at one of the guys to lie the fuck down.

When the chaos in the room settles, I look around and see some of the extended team here to help next to Fire, who is like a raging animal, kicking open doors. Then there's Ice looking like a mean bitch standing over two guys tied up on the ground below her.

What I don't see is that asshole in white. Or Emmy.

"Where the fuck is Emmy?" I scream at Fire to get his attention, and he turns with fury to look at the front door. She's not there, and the door stands open as if we all missed a tiny piece of this fucking puzzle in the middle of that storm.

I race to find her, only to be left with an empty yard of piles of shit against the house. I step into the open and see her around the corner with a white sleeve around her neck. His other arm holds a gun to her head.

My eyes search Emmy's. She's trying to be calm and collected. I know this is hard for one of us to go through, and she's never had any practice in this sort of situation. My heart hurts watching her try to process each breath, knowing it very well may be her last.

"I found her. Would you like to watch me fuck her? I'll let you, since you're my friend." I'm going to kill him. I'm going to fucking kill him. My mind tells me to proceed with caution, but my entire body says he needs to die, and if it means I go here today trying, then so fucking be it. But I won't risk her life.

I don't respond, because that's what he wants me to do. If I feed in to his game, I'm only making it worse for her.

He runs his hands down her shirt, then under the material, and I watch her squirm with disgust. He's put himself in a little grove, with crap all around him, so that no one can get to him from behind. I keep waiting for someone to come around the other side of the house, but they never do.

I take one step toward him. He stiffens up and presses the gun into her temple even harder. "You don't move. I'll shoot her without a fucking thought." I stop moving and watch his face over hers. It's better if I focus on my hatred of him in this instead of what I'm feeling for her right now.

I hear a commotion inside and see Samantha holding Gabriel through the doorway to the house. Okay, mission accomplished. We have what we came for. I know he killed Mallory, and now we have the kid. It's time to end this.

I take a step back this time and hold my hands up in the air in surrender to him. I know by now someone has moved into position to snipe the motherfucker straight off of this earth. "I give up. You can have me. Just let the girl go."

"You think I'm stupid. If I take her, it kills you too."

"But you're fucking wrong there. You killed me already. I died with the other one you killed, so you can't do anything to me today." He smiles a repulsive grin and takes a single step forward, feeling more confident in his position. *Walk forward, motherfucker, walk forward.*

I don't directly watch Emmy's eyes close as I pretty much say she doesn't mean anything to me, even though I know that's not the case as I stand here dying inside because he has her.

Out of nowhere, Emmy leans forward and slaps her hand up, forcing his into the air. She's using defense moves we use in the Army, and it isn't a second later that I hear the shot. Right between his fucking eyes. I know that was Ice, and I hope it gives her the justice I feel instantly. Mallory was her best friend. She's been hurting like I have.

I run to Emmy and pull her into my arms. Her tears and hysteria make me want to hold her tighter, but I have to see he's dead myself. Fire moves to us and pulls Emmy into his arms. I reach for his gun and stand over the Mexican at my feet.

I could put a round of bullets in his body, but the fact of the matter is, none of it will bring Mallory back. He's dead. She's dead. But somehow in the middle of all of this, I've found a second breath of air to prove I'm alive.

I miss her like crazy, and the second Jade comes barreling toward us, I hold her as she cries the hardest I've ever seen her cry. "I hate him. He took her from me, and I'll never get her back."

"I know. He took my entire life away from me. This doesn't seem to be enough justice for what he's done." Just as I finish speaking, Samantha takes a step out of the house. She has Gabriel in her arms, with his head tucked into her neck.

"We have to get them out of here. We don't have time to make sense of all of this now." Kaleb moves toward us, and we both follow him to a van to clear out.

Emmy sits next to me in the seat. I know I need to talk to her, but right now, there's a lump in my throat that won't allow it.

She waits until we've been on the road for a few minutes before she talks to me. "I'm so glad you found your revenge. I'm sorry this had to happen to you." She looks down at her hands, and I still can't make myself form a word. I squeeze her against me and hope she can hear what I can't seem to say out loud.

CHAPTER TWENTY-TWO

HARRIS

The flight home has been strange. I'm trying to process what I'm feeling inside. Everyone is afraid to talk me about anything, which I'm thankful for. I thought killing Mallory's murderer would make me feel better, but it didn't.

I can see the hurt on Emmy's face even though she's busying herself with the young boy. Samantha looks nervous and a bit overwhelmed. I can only imagine what she's going through. She's uprooted her life in the past forty-eight hours, and now she's surrounded by three overbearing people trying to make sure she has everything she needs. She's about to learn what being part of the Maverick family means. It means you gain one hell of an extended family as well. It doesn't matter what a person does in their life. It's how big of a heart you have and how much you're willing to sacrifice for another.

Emmy grounds me in a way I never thought would happen again. She's real and honest, and I would be an absolute fool to not take things slow with her, to see where this could go.

I've made a family with every one of these people. Their love is something that spreads to their close friends as well, but honestly, they are great people. Talk about dedication and loyalty. Kaleb has proven that over and over again, and it just makes me feel at ease knowing Jade found someone like him.

He loves her and she loves him. Life doesn't get any better than that.

Shit. My heart hurts. I don't know how to make the pain stop; it's consumed me for far too long. It's truly eating away at my insides, and I'm on the verge of numb again. My life will never be the same again. I'm not an idiot; I know this, and so does Emmy.

I feel an urge to scream at the top of my lungs until I collapse from pure exhaustion. My mind is warped, confused, and rattling around in my skull, bouncing to the beat of its own lonely drum. She's gone. I will never see Mallory again, and that's something I need to learn to cope with, no matter how hard it is.

I watch Emmy as she cautiously moves closer and places her hand on mine. I know what I said to the guy hurt her, and as soon as I can bring myself to talk, I'm going to tell her I didn't mean it. I would never purposely hurt her. I'm not that guy.

"I'm sorry you're hurting, but I'm here for you." She wraps her arms around my waist, and even though I'm stiff at first, her tight squeeze has me melting against her. I place my arm around her, and we stay like that until we touch down at the compound, all the while listening to Gabriel laugh at Kaleb's ridiculous voices.

That kid is going to have a very loving life. He'll be so damn protected, he'll probably have a tough time getting away with anything fun as a teenager, but he'll be safe nonetheless.

That's the most important thing of all. Happiness, health, and his safety, which he will have and more here.

Jackson, Steele, and Pierce meet us on the runway. It doesn't take half a second for Jackson to zone in on Samantha. I knew she'd be his type. This will be interesting, watching him dance around the compound with actual 'pussy' being allowed, as he calls it. I don't think she's as easy as the one's he's used to though. In fact, I may have to place a bet that she'd give his feisty ass a long run for his money if he even tried to go there.

They all greet us with open arms, and before long, Maverick's mom is with us, crying while she holds a very confused little boy. Samantha stands back and watches from a distance until Gabriel runs to her and begins to ask all kinds of questions. She bends down to his level, her eyes full of love as she explains in great detail who this woman is and what role she would love to play in his life. The two of them are in their own little bubble for a few minutes before Jackson bends down to shake the little guy's hand. He's already got his arm around her and is watching the young boy with adoration.

He stands, lifts the kid up, and stands by Samantha for the Maverick family get-together with a huge fucking smile on his face.

I decide to walk away. Don't get me wrong, I'm happy for all of them. But right now, I just need some time. I start to walk out to the edge of the clearing. This is where I love to run to get away. The view here is amazing, and it's a perfect place to just sit and think about the shit that's built up over this past year.

I'm only there about fifteen minutes when I hear a crackle in the grass. I turn to see Emmy approaching me, and I swallow hard thinking about everything I need to say to her.

She sits down next to me, and we sit in silence for a while. My mind churns with everything I want to tell her, but my mouth can't seem to say any of it, so I finally just say the first thing that comes to mind.

"I loved her. She was supposed to be my forever. Our baby was going to be our forever. My little life was perfect in every aspect until it was all taken away." Her eyes fill with tears, and she leans against me as I continue to talk. She doesn't ask any questions. She just listens to every word I say.

"I haven't told anyone that we had just found out we were going to have a little girl. Mallory was so happy. I was happy. I didn't care what we were having as long as it was healthy." I pause and think about the irony of just wanting a healthy baby. What she would have looked like, what her personality would have been. All of it. "We were going to look at a little dress that day to bring her home in, just in case I was called out on a mission that would keep me away from witnessing her birth. I had no idea I'd never get to see her little face that day. The way her little fingers and toes moved on the screen haunts me every single day." She wipes a tear from her face, and I do the same. She's not looking at me, which somehow makes it easier to spill my most valued memories to her.

"Mallory was full of life. She had a spitfire mouth and wasn't afraid to put me in my place. I wish like hell she could tell me to stop talking and to be able to hold her just one more time." I have to stand. The lump in my throat is suffocating me. I can't talk for a few seconds as I swallow down the painful memories that flash through my mind, but then I continue.

"She was everything to me. When she died, I thought I died. I knew there was nothing left of me to ever love again. I was a shell of a person with barely any will left to live. Then I met you." She swipes her tears again, and I turn to look out at the scenery so I can get all of this out.

"You made me feel alive again. You brought me back to a world where I realize that not everything is gone." I feel like I'm closing in on myself as I continue to talk. I'm trying like hell to make sure these next words come out the exact way I intend them to.

"Shit. I don't know how to say everything I'm thinking. I'm trying to find a way to let go of my past, so I can think about what to do about the future. I didn't mean to hurt you in Mexico. When he talked about hurting you, my gut twisted, and the fear of feeling another loss almost took me to my knees." She stands and walks toward me when I stop talking to fight back the damn tears that won't stop falling from my eyes.

"I don't know what to do with you. Yes, I care about you so much, but I'm still in love with Mallory. How can I ask—"

"Stop," she interrupts me before I have a chance to say anything else. "I don't expect you to feel like you can't love her or miss her. In fact, I'd think less of you if you didn't. I know very well how much she meant to you. I'm not here to make you worry about a future with me. We can just spend time together and see where it takes us." I take in her eyes filled with compassion and strength as she continues to talk around the pain in her heart.

"I hate more than anything you've had to go through all of this. I've come to care about you so much in just a short amount of time, but I'd give it all up to give you the chance to have her again. I see how tortured you are, and I wish like hell I could do something to help you." She leans against my chest and cries out loud. Her beautiful heart pounds against mine. I wrap my arms around her, and we both just hold each other while I finally let it all out.

I haven't cried for Mallory and the baby yet. I've bottled it all up and forced myself to feel everything but what I'm feeling right here. Soldiers don't cry. We kill and get revenge, then we move the fuck on. So why is my face drenched in tears for something I'll never have again?

'You're only human Beau, every human cries. Holding it in isn't good for anyone, son. Let it out.' My mom's words from the day of the funeral ring through my ears and hit me straight in the chest.

Emmy's tight hold on my waist somehow gives me the strength to finally stop the tears and take a deep breath. I think it's my first real deep breath in months.

A bright-blue butterfly flutters around Emmy's hair, and I watch as it lands on her shoulder. She doesn't feel it, but I see it. "You have a bright-blue butterfly on your shoulder." I tell her with a quiver in my voice. She moves slowly to look down at it. A smile splits across her face as she watches it closely until it flies off again.

"Someone once told me a butterfly means a new beginning." She looks at me after she says it. I know she's afraid to push anything with me, and in all reality, I'm not sure what I can handle at this time. But what I do know is, she calms me. She makes me feel alive. And that's something I need in my life.

EPILOGUE

EMMY

Two Weeks Later

"Oh God, Beau. Please."

"That's right, baby. Beg me. Beg me to let you come all over my dick."

To say we're doing well is an understatement. I've spent every second of the last couple of weeks with this man, and every single day is a better one for him. His smile and love of life are returning, and I love that I get to experience this with him. His breakdowns are fewer than they were when we first returned, and Beau is getting stronger every day.

He's learning that his life can go on and that his memories never have to fade away. He's also come to terms with the fact that talking about his loss is something I need as much as he does. I want him to remember her and to always feel that he can come to me when he's having a bad time. But I'll also understand if he needs time to himself.

I've decided to move to the compound for good. Kaleb has plenty of work for me to do here with surveillance, and of course, I have enough medical knowledge to do most of the procedures they need done here. Which is bound to happen more often than not with this crazy, no-holds-barred crew. They're reckless.

Our mom was finally convinced to move here once Gabriel moved in, and it just seemed like the right thing for me to do. Her home in Florida will become our new vacation spot. I can't wait to take my nephew there and show him off to all my friends back home.

Beau was just a cherry on top when I made that decision. I would never make a decision on where to live based on a man, but he didn't hurt my case to live here.

"That's it. So. Deep." He continues to move in me, and if we hadn't already had sex three times today, I'd be selfish to get my release before he gets his. But needless to say, I'm fully satisfied in the sex department.

Something happened to us that day out on the clearing. He changed that day, and since then, we have been different. It's a good different, and I just work to make sure he knows I'm here for him even with his past that's very much a part of our everyday life.

"You feel so good. Feel me slide into that tight pussy of yours. You're so beautiful. Emmy, look at me when I fuck you." He pulls my eyes to his with his words and thrusts harder a few times before slowing his hips again. We watch each other intensely the entire time, which brings me to the edge faster than anything ever has in the past.

"Fuck, Emmy." He bites down on my lips before he sucks the bottom one between his teeth. "Your lips are swollen. I love it when I leave a mark on you. It reminds you where I've been." He's been everywhere. I've been everywhere.

After a few more thrusts, we both moan through our orgasm. I claw my nails into his back as I come down from mine. He knows how to make me insane in the bedroom, and I love it.

"We may have to start sleeping apart so we can actually sleep, you know." I know what his answer will be, but it's fun to tease him anyway.

"Fuck off with that. I'll sleep when I'm dead." We both laugh at his remark.

I don't know what will happen with Beau Harris and me. I only know that right now in this very moment, things couldn't be better. We're living together, and neither one of us has any plans to do anything different. He makes me happy, and by the constant smile on his face, I'd like to think I make him a little happy as well.

Only time will tell if what we have will last, but isn't that the way it is in every relationship? Living with him on this compound will be an adventure of a lifetime, and I can't wait to see what our future holds.

Watch for Book Four in the Elite Forces Series. We promise to give you updates on all of your favorite couples as we move through series!

A special thanks to all of you who have agreed to read this early for us! We hoped you enjoyed this Advanced Reader Copy of Stone and we look forward to hearing what you thought!

Acknowledgments

Hilary Storm

What an adventure this has been! Stone is completely different in this novel and it was fun writing him! I have to thank Kathy first, because when we first started throwing all of this around neither one of us thought this series would be the huge success it is today. We had hoped, but we didn't expect it. It's because of our mutual respect for hard work and the dedication we both put in to our careers that this has been such a great success! So Kathy… thank you for being such a hard worker and loving this as much as I do!

My husband and kids are always the people who have to sacrifice the most when I write. I love them for understanding and challenging me to be even better every time I publish! This was no different!

To Dylan… You have become my sound board and there are so many days that I've almost lost my mind as I'm going in all the different directions… you pull me back and remind me of the reason I need to make certain decisions to ease it all!

Battershell… It was great to finally work with you and Burton on this! That shot is nothing short of AMAZING and perfect for our story! Thank you so much!

Dana... I could NEVER be as awesome as I am without your designs surrounding me! You are hands down the best for me and I love what you do every single time!

Julia and Emma... thanks for cleaning up our mess! It's because of you that it's clean and ready for readers!

Amanda and Lindsey... thank you so much for beta reading this story and giving me your honest feedback. I truly adore that you don't just blow smoke up my ass and tell me you love every word I send you. You look at it with a critical mind and it challenges me to make sure I write better every day. Thank you so much for all you do!

Hall... Thank you for being my blunt friend who is always honest when I need to bounce ideas! Our daily chats save me!

And last but never least... thank you to the readers who are reading this series! It's because of you that we have the demand for another book to follow! Stay tuned because we won't disappoint!

Kathy Coopmans

"We should write a book together, one of us said."

"Let's do it, said the other."

Three books later, one USA today Bestseller and my friend Hilary and I are writing stronger each day. Determined to give you the best we have in this series.

I'm convinced she's my better half in this book world. My friend, confidant, and supporter.

I love writing these characters with her; it's an every day joyful event for the two of us. We laugh, agree, disagree. Mostly, though, we applaud one another. We listen and to me, that is the most important part about collaborating together.

I see many things ahead for this friend and me.

So, Hilary, thank you for showing me how true of a friend you are.

My family. I have the best husband and son's a woman could ask for. Grown men who ask me how my work is going. What did I do today? Am I having fun? It's a repeat process I will never be tired of hearing. They complete me in a way only unconditional love can. I love the three of you so very much.

Jill Sava. My friend, PA, and lifeline. You, my sweet lady, are a brilliant woman. I will keep you!

Eric Battershell and Burton Hughes. I'm never disappointed when you toss a photo my way. You accommodate me, prove to me that every business transaction is important to you. Thank you for showing me a true friendship. I simply adore both of you.

Dana Leah. You are the most patient woman I know. Always changing, jumping on our cover with a fierce determination of professionalism. You work amazes me.

Julia Goda. Our editor. I love you. Enough said!

To our readers, bloggers, and friends. I want to thank you for supportive our fantastic duo. Without those of you who support us we would be strumming our fingers against our temples wondering what in the frick should we do with our lives. You give us the answer, easily. We write, we dream and we create characters that all of us love. Words cannot be written to express how much your support means to me. Thank you from the depths of my soul, the center of my bones for loving the two of us!

BOOKS BY HILARY STORM

Six (Blade and Tori's story)
Seven (Coming Soon)

Rebel Walking Series
In A Heartbeat
Heaven Sent
Banded Together
No Strings Attached
Hold Me Closer
Fighting the Odds
Never Say Goodbye
Whiskey Dreams

Bryant Brothers Series
Don't Close Your Eyes

Alphachat.com Series
Pay for Play
Two can Play

Elite Forces Series
ICE
FIRE
STONE

Stalk Hilary Here
Website: www.hilarystormwrites.com
Facebook: https://www.facebook.com/pages/Hilary-Storm-Author/492152230844841
Goodreads: https://www.goodreads.com/author/show/7123141.Hilary_Storm?from_search=true
Twitter: @hilary_storm
Instagram: http://instagram.com/hilstorm
Tumblr: https://www.tumblr.com/blog/hilarystorm
Snapchat: hilary_storm
Spotify: Hilary Storm

BOOKS BY KATHY COOPMANS

The Shelter Me Series
Shelter Me
Rescue Me
Keep Me

The Syndicate Series
Book one-The Wrath of Cain.
Book two - The Redemption of Roan
Book three - The Absolution of Aiden
Book four - The Deliverance of Dilan:
Book five- Empire

The Drifter

The Contrite Duet
Reprisal

The Elite Forces Series- (Co-written with Hilary Storm)

Stalk Kathy Here

Newsletter- https://app.mailerlite.com/webforms/landing/y3l8t6
Twitter- @authorkcoopmans
Instagram- authorkathycoopmans
FB- https://www.facebook.com/AuthorKathyCoopmans/
www.authokathycoopmans